Trouble In NEW YORK

SYLVIA BISHOP

Illustrated by Mar___ G_____lupi

SCHOLASTIC

Scholastic Children's Books
An imprint of Scholastic Ltd
Euston House, 24 Eversholt Street, London, NW1 1DB, UK
Registered office: Westfield Road, Southam, Warwickshire, CV47 0RA
SCHOLASTIC and associated logos are trademarks and/or
registered trademarks of Scholastic Inc.

First published in the UK by Scholastic Ltd, 2019

ISBN 978 1407 18441 8

A CIP catalogue record for this book
is available from the British Library.

Printed by CPI Group (UK) Ltd, Croydon, CR0 4YY
Papers used by Scholastic Children's Books are made
from wood grown in sustainable forests.

1 3 5 7 9 10 8 6 4 2

This is a work of fiction. Names, characters, places, incidents
and dialogues are products of the author's imagination or are used
fictitiously. Any resemblance to actual people, living or dead,
events or locales is entirely coincidental.

www.scholastic.co.uk

To the good ship 9a, and all who have sailed in her

READERS INTRODUCED TO NEW YORK PAPERBOY

Before Jamie Creeden wrote the news, he used to deliver it.

Every morning before school, he would wake in the dark and make his own breakfast while his mother slept. He would head out through that darkness on his bicycle to Lou Moon's store and collect his newspapers. Then he would ride through the gathering dawn, down the straight wide streets, tearing round their sharp corners, delivering the *Morning Yorker* to the tower blocks and town houses of Brooklyn, New York City.

He always pedalled as fast as he could. If he finished

1

early enough, he would have time to buy a warm pretzel from the cart near his school, sit on the wall next to the cart and read a copy of the *Yorker* from cover to cover. If it was raining or snowing, the pretzel seller would lend him a big black umbrella to sit under, to keep the paper dry.

By the time the school bell rang each morning, Jamie knew everything that was happening in the world that day. He knew what they were saying from Texas to Alaska; what they were doing from Rome to Russia to Rio. And once he had all that information inside him, not to mention the pretzel, it didn't seem to matter so much what eighty-one divided by nine was, or how you spelled M-I-S-S-I-S-S-I-P-P-I, or whether Bruce Rankin thought his haircut was stupid.

Jamie's teachers sometimes wished that he cared a *little* bit more what eighty-one divided by nine was. But they gave up trying too hard to enthuse him. Jamie Creeden was never going to be a numbers man. Jamie Creeden was going to write the news.

He had always been very sure about this, even though his spelling was often a bit improvised, and no one in his family wore sharp suits and shiny shoes like the reporters he admired. He just went ahead and knew it anyway.

And this is the story of how – quite unexpectedly – he turned out to be right.

PAPERBOY MEETS HERO

26 June 1969

It was late June. The city sweltered, and most of the summer vacation still lay ahead, as long and golden as evening light. It was Jamie's favourite time of year.

Today, like every summer day, he planned to do three things:

1. Deliver and read the news in the
   Morning Yorker.
2. Investigate and write the news for his Young
   Reporter of the Year entry.

3. Go to Pepe's diner and watch the nine o'clock news on *Goodnight, New York*. (With chocolate milkshake.)

It was a lot to do, so before sun and city were awake, Jamie was pedalling to Lou Moon's store to collect his papers.

He had learned to slow down when he arrived at Lou's store, and to enter as gently as he could. He had learned, eventually, to catch the door behind him, and make sure that it didn't bang. But however gentle he was, the bell still tinkled.

"Tinkle," muttered Lou. "Tinkle tinkle, every morning. That boy's got no consideration for an old man's ears." Lou always muttered. His mouth was turned down from long years of muttering, and his moustache flopped down with it, and his long nose drooped over them both like an awning.

"Good morning," said Jamie.

"Is it?" said Lou. He sneezed morosely.

"Bless you."

"Too late for that," sighed Lou, "I'm already sick.

Perry's sick too. Just called to say he's staying in bed. Wish *I* could stay in bed." He shook his head, and repeated sadly, "Too late."

Jamie nodded sympathetically, but he wasn't really thinking about Lou. He was thinking about Perry, who was the other paperboy. "Who's doing the other route then?"

Lou shrugged. He sneezed again, with extra woe, before replying, "Nobody."

"But," said Jamie, "the *Yorker* is always punctual!" And this was true. Adverts across the city showed the smiling face of the editor, Harry Hooper, with the words "ALWAYS PUNCTUAL. OFTEN ACCURATE" written in big red letters. It was a promise: people could rely on the *Morning Yorker* to reach their doormats by seven thirty without fail. That was the secret of its success. While TV news was taking over, and newspapers up and down the country were going bust, the *Yorker* was more popular than ever – and just last Christmas, Harry Hooper himself had sent a bar of chocolate to all the paperboys and papergirls, to thank them for keeping the *Yorker* punctual.

But Lou just shrugged again, indifferent.

Jamie thought fast. He cared deeply about the *Yorker*; and besides, two routes meant twice the pay. He picked up the extra bundle of papers. "I could do the second route," he said. "After mine."

Lou's eyes widened. Jamie's enthusiasm baffled him. But then, everything about this boy baffled Lou, from his unreasonable morning energy to his unreasonably red hair. "Sure," he said, "if you want. Don't see why anyone would want to." He thought about this for a few seconds, then concluded, "Strange kid."

Jamie was not around to hear this assessment of himself. He had rushed out at "if you want", because he *did* want, and there wasn't a moment to lose.

He did his own route in record time, throwing papers wildly on to stoops, screeching around corners and upsetting clouds of starlings that had gathered on the pavements. When the last paper had been thrown he went screeching and starling-bothering onwards to Perry's route.

By now there were a few early morning dog walkers. He was much slower this time, because he didn't know the route, and kept pausing to check Lou's list. Also, he

7

accidentally threw a paper at a jogger's head, and had to stop and apologize for ages.

He reached the last house at 7.32, which wasn't bad. It was in the posh part of the neighbourhood, which wound along the waterfront. Here there were big detached houses with front lawns, which looked out across the water to Staten Island, hazy in the morning light.

The last house was the biggest and front-lawn-iest of the lot. He threw down their paper triumphantly, and stood gasping for breath by his bike. All the rushing had made him feel a bit sick, and his face had turned the colour of his hair.

He was so busy gasping that he stopped paying attention for a minute. He didn't hear the doorway of the house opening. He didn't notice when somebody stepped out on to the lawn, picked up the paper, and watched him silently – head on one side, considering.

"You're not the usual boy," they said.

Jamie turned his head, opening his mouth to reply; and then left it open. The someone on the porch was none other than Harry Hooper, editor of the *Morning*

Yorker. Wearing a striped dressing gown.

"You're two minutes late," he went on. He didn't shout – he didn't need to. You could tell just by the way he *stood* how important he was. His dressing gown was swirling about a bit in the breeze, but somehow, he made it look dignified.

"The paper mustn't be late," he explained, his eyes full of gentle disappointment. "It's very important. It's the one thing I quite insist on."

"Yes – sir – but – Perry's – sick," wheezed Jamie. He was still struggling to breathe normally, so it sounded more like "Hessah, Pearzick". Harry Hooper's head went back down on one side, into considering position.

"Are you all right there, kid?"

Jamie took an almighty lungful, and managed, "Sir. Just out of breath. Had to do two routes."

"Two routes? Why?"

So Jamie explained, as best he could with his gulping lungs. Harry kept his head on one side through the whole story. When Jamie had finished, he righted his head, and smiled.

"Well," he said, "I owe you an apology, kid. I was

ticking off the wrong boy. Turns out you're the hero of the hour."

"Sir," said Jamie. He didn't know what else to say.

Now that he had got his breath back, it was finally dawning on him that this was his *chance*. He was standing in front of *the* most important man in the news business. The man who had the ear of everyone from the president to the mayor to the chief of police; the man who ran the last daily paper still thriving in New York; the man who could make or break a reporter's career. And so far, he had spent most of the conversation panting at him.

He was running out of time. As if in a dream, he could hear that Harry was thanking him for being such a fine and dedicated paperboy – and turning away, towards the door...

"I'm a reporter as well as a paperboy, Mr Hooper," said Jamie quickly (and a bit too loudly). "I started our school paper. It's called the *Bay Ridge Bugle*. I do local news but I do investigations and stuff too, and I write up world news, and some of the neighbours take it now as well, and..." He took the plunge. "I want to work for the *Yorker*, one day."

Harry chuckled. "Well, I'm glad to hear it!" he said. And he chuckled some more, but by the time he had finished chuckling, Jamie had produced a *Bay Ridge Bugle* from his bag to show him; and when he had flicked through a couple of pages, he wasn't chuckling any more. He began turning the pages more slowly.

"This," he said at last, "is not bad."

Jamie made a noise that might have meant thank you, but then again, might have meant pretty much anything at all.

"Not bad at all, kid. Say," said Harry – and his eyes lit up with pleasure at his own idea – "would you like to come and see the *Yorker* offices sometime? Meet a few of the reporters, if you like?"

Jamie stared at Harry Hooper as though he was seeing Father Christmas himself. In June. In a dressing gown. Then he remembered to speak again, and said, "Yes! Please. I would. Yes."

"Swell. That'd be swell. How about I take a telephone number from you, and I'll give you a call?" Harry took a fountain pen from his dressing-gown pocket and handed it to Jamie, along with his copy of the *Yorker*.

As neatly as he could, in the top margin of the front page, Jamie printed JAMIE CREEDEN (PAPERBOY), and his phone number and address.

"Swell," said Harry, tucking the newspaper under his arm. "I'll be in touch. You go home and have a well-earned rest, kid."

"Thank you, Mr Hooper," said Jamie.

"Thank *you*." And raising his hand in farewell, he disappeared back into his house and shut the door.

For a second or two Jamie just stared at the spot where he had been. Then he punched the air, jumped on to his bicycle and raced off into his day.

It had been a huge day already, and Jamie hadn't even finished point one on his plan. He still had to read the news, write the news and watch the news. But first, he stopped off back home. He usually cycled back via Mrs Darling's; he used to help out with her front garden, and now she always let him pick a flower for his mom. By this time of morning his mom had left for her job at the launderette, and she wouldn't be home until she had finished her second job at the restaurant. If she worked the late shift then Jamie might be in bed when she got back, and not see her at all. This made her feel very guilty, and she was forever dreaming up terrible things that might happen to him and convincing herself that it would be her own fault for leaving him alone all day – as though she had any choice. So he always left a flower and a note, to say hello.

This morning it was a particularly long and scribbly note, reporting everything that had happened with Harry Hooper. Then he loaded up his satchel with his notebook and pens and lunch, and set off again.

His second stop was Memorial Pier, his favourite spot in the whole city. It was on the edge of Long Island, so he could sit there and look across the water to the shore of Manhattan Island, where a string of skyscrapers winked and sparkled in the sunlight. Here, he read the paper.

So far, this year had been a roller coaster of astonishing headlines. Protests and riots, revolutions and wars, Concorde airplanes and space rockets and satellites... Even right here in New York, there had been a string of strange crimes, which were thrilling and baffling everyone in equal measure. Every morning Jamie would find that half the people on the pier were reading the *Yorker*, and the other half were gossiping about it.

Today's headline was no exception. A big-deal Russian actress had vanished from her dressing room, right before the first performance of her solo show in the USA. The paper had been trumpeting her arrival for weeks. It was a major scandal, and the police had no idea how it had been done. After that there was nothing much new, but Jamie read it all anyway, right up to the adverts at the back.

Once the paper had been thoroughly read, he turned to task two: his own reporting. He had one more week to perfect his Young Reporter of the Year article. Jamie wanted to win the Young Reporter more than anything. The winner had their piece published on the front page of the *Yorker*, and then after that they were allowed to write a column for the *Yorker* every Sunday for a whole year; plus there was a cash prize, and when Jamie had told his mom how much it was she had choked on her coffee. It had got a bit out of hand, actually, and Jamie had to thump her on the back for ages, and all the coffee had ruined her good dress. But he decided there and then that he was going to win.

That was three years ago, and for three years Jamie hadn't won. Last year it had gone to a boy called Sidney Blake, who interviewed none other than the president of the United States. His dad was best mates with the president, and they all went sailing together every summer. It was hard for Jamie to compete with that.

This year, though, Jamie was definitely going to win. His friend Pepe, who ran the Bay Ridge Diner, had given him his scoop: all the diners in New York were going on strike that August, to protest about a new tax on their milkshakes. They hadn't gone to the press yet, so Jamie would be the first person to write about it. It was an *exclusive* scoop.

So Jamie spent the day pedalling from diner to diner, persuading people to talk to him. It kept him out late; by the time he was cycling back to Pepe's for his final stop of the day, the sky had darkened and the water had turned black. Over the river's surface the street lights cast stripes of gold, and the ships' lights cast stripes of white and green. The edges of the other islands glittered with more lights of their own.

Jamie didn't pause to look, because he was almost

late for his nightly TV viewing at Pepe's. He charged through the door extra fast to make up for it.

"Ah," said Pepe, "the cacophonic noise of my favourite customer." He looked up from the table he was cleaning and smiled at Jamie. He always made Jamie think of an upside-down exclamation mark, with his long thin body and his excited little dot of a head. They were old friends, and Pepe loved the world of news reporting almost as much as Jamie.

"Hello," said Jamie. He hopped on to a stool by the counter and swivelled it round until he was dizzy. "Hey, Pepe – you'll never guess who I met today."

"Well, if I'll never guess," said Pepe, leaning on his countertop, "you'll have to tell me."

"*Harry Hooper!*"

"WHAT?"

So Jamie told the whole story. Pepe was so delighted that he made Jamie two free milkshakes at once to celebrate. He had a hundred questions; at around the eighty-fifth, Jamie had to remind him to turn on the television for the start of *Goodnight, New York*.

Pepe rolled his eyes, but he was still smiling. "You

must be the only person who still bothers watching *Goodnight, New York* after they've read the paper," he said. "Miss Bell is losing her touch. She never says anything I haven't already read in the *Yorker*."

"She's still good," said Jamie loyally. So they turned on the TV, and Jamie started on his second milkshake, and watched the world unfold on the screen.

It was true that the show was a disappointment these days. It used to be brilliant – the reporter, Cindy Bell, was somehow always one step ahead of everybody else. She was so popular that every daily paper in New York had closed, besides the *Yorker*. But recently, it felt lazy. Cindy still delivered the show with style: with her white-blonde hair swirled up on top of her head, she looked like a very serious Mr Whippy ice cream. But she had nothing on the actress story that hadn't been in the paper – no interviews, no investigation, nothing.

She did have *one* new scoop, which she saved right for the end. When Jamie heard it, he froze mid-slurp, milkshake suspended in the straw.

Cindy turned to the camera with an especially serious

face. "And now," she said, "some bad news for the summer. Diners are set to strike this August over a tax hike on their milkshakes. We went out into the city to find out more…"

Jamie and Pepe gaped at the television in horrified silence, watching as Cindy interviewed a glum diner manager. They were still gaping as the closing music played. They slowly un-gaped as the advertisements began, but neither spoke. What was there to say? That was meant to be Jamie's big scoop – and Cindy had got there first.

Pepe turned the television off. The diner felt very quiet.

"Someone leaked it early," said Jamie, finally. "They *leaked* it."

"Oh, Jamie," said Pepe, laying a comforting hand on his arm. "You can still submit your story."

"It won't be the same," said Jamie miserably. "I need to stand out. This was *my* story. And I've only got a week left now."

Pepe sighed. This was all true. So he just said, "Another chocolate milkshake?"

"Yes, please," said Jamie. "Thanks, Pepe." He slumped his chin into his hands.

A minute later Pepe put the foaming glass of milkshake down in front of him and looked him squarely in the eyes. He was six foot seven, so this involved doubling himself almost in half to lean on the counter and get his eyes level with Jamie's, but he did it with great dignity. "Now listen. You are going to win," he said. "You met Harry Hooper this morning, remember? And he saw something in you – something that will make a great reporter. He invited you into his newsroom! You're going *inside* the *Yorker* headquarters, and who knows what you'll see there! I guarantee you, by the end of your day there you will have an idea. You will have *the* idea."

Jamie nodded. He was still disappointed, but it wasn't in his nature to stay sad for very long: it involved too much sitting still. So he un-slumped his chin, took a slurp of his milkshake and said, "Thanks, Pepe. Yeah. I'll figure it out. I guess I *might* find an idea at the *Yorker.*"

And this guess, as it happened, was overwhelmingly correct.

In a way.

YORKER HEADQUARTERS REVEALED

29 June 1969

The next day, Harry Hooper didn't call. It was the longest day Jamie had ever known, ever. He began to think Harry must have forgotten all about him. Or changed his mind. Or fallen in the Narrows.

He delivered the news and read the news, as usual (more about the missing actress: the pier buzzed with gossip). He didn't report the news because he didn't have any new ideas, unless you counted his neighbour

Barry suggesting for the twenty-seventh time that he should write about the Unacceptable Situation with the Trash Collection.

When it was time to watch the news on *Goodnight, New York*, Pepe gave him three up-cheering milkshakes. But he still didn't cheer up. First, he was sad because Harry Hooper still hadn't called. And second, he was sad because the network had decided that *Goodnight, New York* wasn't doing well enough, and now half of Cindy Bell's hour had been given to another news anchor, who ran a piece about super-intelligent ladybugs being used as communist spies. It was obviously nonsense. But it was probably good for ratings.

Back home, he tried taking the phone off the hook and putting it back on again, in case there was something wrong with it. This didn't seem to help. So he went to bed.

But then, the next morning, Harry Hooper called.

He called while Jamie's mom was still asleep, which made her say "Wuuuurghaargh" gently to herself. And he invited Jamie to visit the *Yorker* the very next day. Jamie said lots of polite "Yes, sirs" and "Thank you, sirs", while doing a small jig and getting himself a bit tangled in the phone cord. Then he put his head round his mom's door to tell her; but she had rolled over and gone back to sleep, and he didn't like to wake her. So he just told himself, over and over again, as he went pedalling around the city. The next day he woke an hour early out of sheer excitement, and had to wait impatiently in his hot little room for the day to start. Then he made himself breakfast in the dark, as usual; did his route, as usual; picked a flower for his mom, as usual; and read the paper on the pier, as usual.

The headline was spectacular, but even so, Jamie found it hard to concentrate. ARSONIST STRIKES AGAIN, it read. The Arsonist was a mysterious figure who had been burning buildings in New York all summer. Every time, he would stay amongst the flames playing a haunting melody on his violin, before vanishing safely at the last moment. Up and down the pier, people were gossiping about his latest attack: the excitement with the actress was already forgotten. But all Jamie could concentrate on was his watch, slowly slicing the morning away.

At last it was time. He went home, put on his good shirt, wafted a comb in the direction of his hair and set out on the long bike ride to Midtown Manhattan.

In Midtown there is very little space left to build sideways, so people build upwards. The *Yorker* building was twenty-three storeys tall, and crenellated at the top like a castle turret. Over the door were the words *Semper punctualis, saepe vero* – which is Latin (sort of) for "Always punctual, often accurate" – and a statue of a woman. In one hand the woman held a lantern, for Truth; and in the other, a Rolex watch, for Punctuality. (She used to hold an hourglass, but the Rolex company paid the *Yorker* a great deal of money to change it.)

It was the sort of building designed to make you feel a bit timid. Fortunately, Jamie never stood still long enough to notice things like that, and *fwmph*-ed happily through the revolving doors without stopping to worry about virtuous statues or unnecessary Latin.

Inside, though, he paused.

The light was strange: that was the first thing he noticed. It was a warm, golden light, and it seemed to come from everywhere at once.

The second thing he noticed was the one-hundred-foot-tall candle.

It stood in the centre of the room, a great trunk of wax, kept inside a glass tunnel that stretched all the way to the bronze ceiling at the very top of the building. Above the ground floor, the next twenty-two floors ran around the edges of the building, leaving a square gap in the centre for the candle.

Gold rails lined each floor, and there was another on the spiral staircase that wound its way around the candle's glass case. The ceilings were all made of engraved bronze. With all that gold-and-bronze going on, the light was bounced and thrown and reflected around so many times that the whole place seemed to be casting light.

There was a very normal receptionist at a very normal desk in front of the giant candle. She looked faintly bored, as though being the guardian of a fiery monolith of wax was getting a bit old. She waited politely for Jamie to stop gawping. When he didn't, she asked, "Can I help you?"

"Hello," said Jamie. "I have an appointment with Harry Hooper. Twelve o'clock."

Tremendously bored by this, the receptionist phoned Harry, then made a heroic effort to smile at Jamie. "He's in a meeting, and he says you should join him," she said. "One A.M."

"Um," said Jamie, glancing at his watch, "on the phone he said midday…"

"One A.M.," she said, "is the top floor." She gestured vaguely. "The elevator's broken. You'll have to take the stairs."

Jamie was bursting with questions, but the receptionist did not seem like a fan of questions, and he was in danger of being late if he had to climb all those stairs. So he bottled the questions up for now and took the stairs two at a time, round and round and round. About halfway up he reached the top of the candle, and the light was fierce. There was a liquid pool of wax around the flame, which ran in rivers down the candle's edge. Above him a mighty plume of smoke rose up inside the glass.

He reached the top floor at eleven fifty-nine. He took a few enormous lungfuls of air. Then he set out to find

Harry Hooper's meeting.

This was not difficult. The rabble of voices coming from inside were all talking at the kind of volume that got Jamie sent out of class *at once*.

He knocked.

"Come in!" called a voice.

Jamie took one more gulping breath, and opened the door. A table of faces all turned towards him. He swallowed and took a step into the room.

"Well, well, it's my finest employee, right on time!" said Harry. He was wearing a suit now, not a striped dressing gown, but he still wore the same gently dignified air. "Come on in, Jamie, come on in. Gentlemen, this is Jamie Creeden, our heroic paperboy. Jamie, meet my senior reporters." He swept an arm across the room, where a pack of slick-haired men were poised mid-argument. They all smiled a hello, and Harry introduced them one by one. Jamie knew all the names from the *Yorker*'s lead articles: Rod Wilder and Ted Malone and Bud Finkleby and Todd Hunter-Bun and Ed Gosh and Judd Minkfort and Ned Parry Junior and Chad M. D'Chad.

It was strange seeing them all in the same room, a

matching set of well-oiled heads and shiny shoes and firm handshakes. They were a bit *too* matching. He was suddenly very conscious of his old shoes and his messy hair. "Hello," he said.

"Take a seat, Jamie," said Harry. "We're just having our daily check-in. Help yourself to a cookie. Now, Bud, have you got anything more on that missing actress…?"

So Jamie sat down and took a fancy cookie, and watched in fascination. The reporters all paced about and pounded the table and sketched ideas in the air with their hands. Harry sat in the middle, inviting one to speak with a nod, silencing another with a wave of his hand, and listening to everyone with his head on one side, considering.

All the reporters were still buzzing about the Arsonist, and Harry had to keep interrupting to get them back on topic. There was so much, he reminded them, to be discussed; and he wasn't wrong. As well as the Arsonist, there was the continued search for the missing actress; the progress of plans to send a man to the moon; the ongoing war in Vietnam; riots up in Greenwich Village. . . The men all talked at double speed, and Jamie could see why. They had to fit the whole world inside their meeting.

Finally Harry showed everyone a graph that showed how much *Yorker* sales were going up, and they all cheered; then he showed them another graph that showed how much more he wanted them to go up, and they all looked serious and nodded; and then he showed them a third graph which was to do with something called profit margins, and Ned Parry Junior had to be gently nudged awake by Todd Hunter-Bun.

At last Harry turned to Jamie and said, "Well, you see how it is here, kid – hectic! Any questions so far?"

There were so many, but one had been bottled up inside him from the moment he arrived, so he chose that one first. "Yes," he said. "What's up with the enormous candle?"

Rod and Ted and Bud and Todd and Ed and Judd and Ned and Chad all laughed, and Harry raised his eyes to the heavens. "You might well ask, kid," he said. "My father, George Hooper, likes tradition. He's still editor-in-chief, you see. And he won't hear of removing it. The candle stands for truth, of course – and that *particular* candle is a timepiece. Ever heard of a candle clock? Well, that's the biggest candle clock in the world. Every day, we have another twenty-four hours of news to deal with. And every day, that candle burns down at a speed of precisely one hour per storey: twenty-four, including the basement. Up here, we're at One A.M."

This was astonishing. Jamie was duly astonished. "Then what? What happens when it's all burned out?"

"We light a new one," said Harry. "Half a million papers are picked up here at midnight, on the *dot*, every night. And as the papers leave, all thirty press workers help pour in the wax for a new candle."

"Wow," said Jamie. "That must cost a fortune."

"It does," sighed Harry. "Luckily, the Hoopers also own a candle company. And speaking of my crazy family, Eve should be here by now. Her mother wanted her to take the tour. Again." He looked at his watch. "I was expecting her to be late, but even for Eve this is something. I'm afraid she's very brilliant," he explained apologetically – then, raising his voice to the room at large, he said, "Has anybody seen Eve?"

None of the reporters had. Harry checked his watch

impatiently a few times, which didn't help. He had just started saying, "Well, kid, maybe we should—" when the door opened at last.

A girl of about Jamie's age came in. She was tall, and stooped gently forward. She wore an expensive blue dress, but the right-hand side was badly singed, and she smelled strongly of smoke. Her mousy curls were shorter on the right than on the left, and the ends of the shortened curls were still smouldering gently.

"Hello, Uncle Harry," she said. "Oooh," she added, "cookies." And she drifted over, picked one up, and started eating it.

Rod and Ted and Bud and Todd and Ed and Judd and Ned and Chad all looked at her, then at each other, then at Harry.

"Eve," said Harry gravely. "You *know* your mother doesn't approve of fire. Well, dare I ask what happened?"

Eve looked at him with slight surprise, as though she had forgotten he was there. "Oh," she said. "Your elevator was broken, so I fixed it."

"I see. Did this involve you setting fire to my elevator?"

"Well, it set itself on fire, really," she said. "The covers on your wires had frayed. You should check that regularly. Electricity through bare wire is a fire hazard." And she munched her cookie thoughtfully. Jamie reckoned this was probably the least of the building's problems. He wondered if Eve had maybe not seen the enormous hundred-foot flame tower.

There was a brief pause. "I see," Harry said, eventually. "Well, Eve, meet Jamie. He wants to be a reporter."

Eve bobbed her head about in a friendly hello, like a (slightly burnt) flower bobbing on its stalk. She gave him a surprisingly sharp, appraising look, and suddenly he felt she might be nowhere near as vague as she seemed. But then the look was gone again as quickly as it had come, and her head carried on bobbing, as though she had got distracted by a thought mid-bob and forgotten to stop.

"Now," said Harry, "I promised you kids a tour. I was hoping to take you around myself, but the mayor has asked to take me out for lunch. Again. The trouble with running the most influential paper in the United States,

Jamie, is that everybody from the president down wants to have lunch with you." He sighed elegantly. "So, I've got to go, but I've got a real treat for you kids. One of my very top reporters has the morning free…" And Harry beckoned Bud Finkleby over. "You still OK to give these kids the tour, Bud?"

"Sure thing," said Bud, winking down at Jamie, and smiling a smile that revealed a winking gold tooth. Bud was … shiny. His hair oil was inches thick, and he had even oiled his thin moustache. This was, Jamie thought, a mistake. It looked like a slimy tadpole had been glued to his upper lip.

"Swell," said Harry. "Swell. Um. Eve. Why are you under the table?"

Eve came out from under the table, where she seemed to be examining its joints, and smiled vaguely at Harry. With a sigh, he said his goodbyes and left; the reporters followed him out. Jamie and Eve were left alone with Bud Finkleby.

"Right!" said Bud, smoothing his moustache. "Let's take the tour!"

A fly tried to land on Bud's head, skittered helplessly

in his hair oil, and slid off again in dismay. When Jamie had imagined meeting his heroes, he hadn't imagined them being quite so shiny. But Bud was an amazing reporter, with more front pages than anybody else, so Jamie forgave him for his shininess, and followed him out to see the rest of the headquarters.

He had never known that there were so many rooms involved in making a newspaper.

They began by taking the elevator down to the reporter's floors, which stretched from Nine P.M. up to Five P.M.

"Well, this is where it all happens, kids," said Bud. "The last great New York daily. Every single man here works heroically hard to get our papers out into the world." And he yawned enormously, leaned on a nearby desk and took a pot of oil from his pocket to touch up his moustache.

Eve and Jamie exchanged glances. Bud didn't *seem* like he was working heroically hard.

Re-oiled, he took them around the desks, introducing them to everybody. All the other reporters were very friendly, and let Jamie try out their typewriters and record himself on their Dictaphones and so on. One even let Eve break apart and reassemble his typewriter.

Jamie loved these rooms. They were thick with the clatter of typewriter keys and the smell of coffee. There was always something new arriving, via the ringing telephones or the canisters of paper that appeared with a *fwop* through the pneumatic tubes. Through the large glass windows, the candle cast strange pools of light and shade, reminding everybody to hurry. Jamie never wanted to leave.

But eventually it was time to move on. They took the stairs, winding round and round the candle. From Four P.M. to Three P.M. it was the editors' floors, where the reporters' work was corrected in red pen; then from Two P.M. to One P.M., the researchers. They drank even more coffee than the reporters.

"We make sure the reporters have all the information they need," one researcher explained to Jamie, while Eve played with a fax machine and Bud had a quick nap at one of the desks. "And we find them leads – that's anyone they can talk to who might know something."

"We don't even know what it is we're chasing half the

time," complained another. "We just know *something's* up, so we chase it. Leads are like Russian dolls: they just keep leading you to the next one."

"And meanwhile," added another, "the flickering of that candle never stops. It gets worst here around mid-afternoon, just when you're starting to *really* panic."

"On this floor," sighed a third, "we have our own motto: always punctual, even if it kills you." The second researcher gently woke the first, who had fallen asleep in her coffee.

The heart of the building, Midday, was Harry Hooper's personal floor. Jamie had no idea what he could want a whole floor for. Eleven A.M. was the photo room, complete with a darkroom, a small room in complete blackness where the film from the backs of cameras could be turned into prints using special chemicals. Then at Ten A.M., the wire room, where telex machines juddered and spluttered out reams of paper with the latest news, wired in from all over the world. The noise here was astonishing.

"These things never stop, hey!" said Bud. "Sometimes I wish I could just wire the world back and say, hey, chill out a minute, huh? You know?"

Jamie didn't know, and Eve didn't care, so there was an awkward little silence.

"Well," said Bud, "that's nearly everything. After this floor it's all admin upstairs, real boring. Hey, I know. Let's go down to Midnight. You'll like this in particular, little lady," he said to Eve.

Eve smiled one of those useful bland smiles that might mean anything at all, and they all took the elevator down to the basement.

In the basement, they met a huge man in overalls called Hal. There were two rooms here. One was mostly filled with lines of tall, thin machines, with keyboards and stools attached to the front.

"Linotype machines!" said Hal. "These keyboards aren't typing on paper – they're typing on to bars of lead. Then we arrange the lead on trays, and use them to make a metal mould of the day's newspaper. Quite something, huh?" He grinned at them. "And *then* the metal moulds are used in the printer – follow me."

He took them through to the second room, which housed the most enormous machine Jamie had ever seen. It was lined with ladders running up to a balcony, in case you wanted to reach the top of it. The sides were blue metal, and riddled with wheels and levers. "Here she is!" cried Hal – and he showed them where you put the metal copy you had made, slotted on to enormous rollers inside the machine, where it would press inky letters on to the pages. The thousands of finished newspapers were then lifted out to the delivery room by conveyor belts, which criss-crossed overhead.

"Always punctual!" said Hal. "Those papers have got to get all over the state by dawn; if we're late in here the whole chain goes wrong, and they won't be there to go out with our paperboys and papergirls – kids like you, Joey," he concluded, clapping Jamie fondly on the back.

Hal was very proud of the machines, and delighted by all Eve's questions about them. "Everything here is the very best of its kind," he said, patting his belly proudly, as though his belly was somehow responsible for them. "You kids should see us down here when we're in action. It's quiet here now, but boy, it isn't quiet then." He rapped on the press. "This machine can do two hundred thousand copies an hour! Two hundred thousand! And it gets a sharper print quality than any other press around – you should take a look at the quality of our photos. Now, the Printagogo 3000 *does* have a more reliable reel tension paster, but *I* find—"

Bud tried and failed to hide a yawn. "Quite something, Hal," he said. "Watch what you say, or this little lady will be wanting to take it apart."

"That so, Eve?" Hal smiled. "You like machines, huh?"

Eve nodded. "And other things too, anything you can build," she said. "Bridges and tunnels are my favourite. I'm going to be an engineer."

Bud laughed, his moustache tadpole writhing about. "An engineer, huh! And Jamie here a reporter. You kids!" Nobody else laughed, because nothing was really funny, so Bud laughed extra loudly to make up for it. Then he looked at his watch and said, "Say, Hal, how about you show our engineer around the machines a bit, huh? There's something I'd like to show our young reporter."

"Um," said Jamie. But Bud was already steering him by the elbow. As he looked back, Eve made a face at Bud's back, and it was so impressively grotesque that Jamie nearly laughed out loud. But he didn't, because Bud's grip on his elbow was a bit painfully tight. He heard Hal beginning to explain the parts of the linotype, then the elevator doors slid open, and he was being steered inside.

When the doors had shut, Bud let Jamie go.

"So, here's the deal," he said, smoothing his moustache with one finger. "You want to have a go at being a real reporter, pal?"

Jamie nodded cautiously.

"Well, kid, are you in for a treat, hey? Here's the thing. I got a note, promising me a phone call with a big scoop about that missing actress – Irena Dragunova – you read about her? Well, this lady didn't say what time she was gonna call, but she said she was only gonna call once, and I had better be waiting by the phone." Bud rolled his eyes. "Crazy. I get crackpots like this calling all the time. The trouble is, I have to take their crazy calls, because one in every hundred crackpots turns out to have a scoop – and the boss'd be mad if I miss something." He leaned in a little closer. "Now, truth is, what I'd *like* to be doing this evening is meeting an old pal of mine. And *you*'d like to be a reporter. So how about you sit and take the call? Pretend to be me, and write down whatever she tells you? You can play with the typewriter and all that. Waddya think?"

What Jamie thought was that Bud was the most useless lazy reporter of all time, and it was astonishing that he had written so many front pages. But he didn't say this, because he *did* want this chance, a lot. So he hid his thoughts, and nodded.

"Great," said Bud. "Great. You come up with me, then, I'll get you sorted. Maybe don't tell anyone why you're there, hey? Just say I let you play around, but don't mention the call. I've got a reputation to keep!"

With a *ding*, the elevator arrived at Six P.M. Bud steered Jamie to the right desk. Jamie sat. In front of him lay the typewriter, telephone, Dictaphone, notebooks and pens, all with the flame-and-hourglass *Yorker* crest, all laid out neatly. Around him, the heads of other reporters bobbed about behind piles of paper.

Above him, Bud grinned down, gold tooth winking.

"Great. Use whatever you want here, kid, knock yourself out. And leave me a note about the call, huh?" He patted Jamie on the shoulder. "You enjoy yourself."

Then, just like that, Bud Finkleby hurried away, and Jamie Creeden was left to swivel in the chair of the New York City correspondent of the *Morning Yorker*.

He breathed in the lingering smell of coffee, and listened to the thin fast tapping of the reporters who hadn't yet finished their stories, and thought about all the wonderful rooms he had seen. Bud Finkleby was an idiot. But he had made Jamie very happy.

He read the note Bud had been left, and tingled all over at the thought that soon *he* would be taking the call:

MR FINKLEBY,

I HAVE INFORMATION ABOUT IRENA DRAGUNOVA. I SAW WHAT REALLY HAPPENED THAT DAY. THERE WAS NO MAGIC TRICK: THIS IS THE REAL WORLD, AND REAL PEOPLE DON'T JUST VANISH INTO THIN AIR!

I WILL CALL YOU TONIGHT, BUT I WILL ONLY BE ABLE TO CALL ONCE, AND I DON'T KNOW WHEN. PLEASE BE BY YOUR TELEPHONE TO TAKE THE CALL. YOU DON'T WANT TO MISS THIS!

YOURS IN GOOD FAITH.

His first scoop. He carefully folded the note and placed it back on the desk, before putting his fingers on the keys of the typewriter and hammering out:

By Jamie Creeden

It looked just as good as he had always imagined it would.

Then Bud's telephone rang.

PAPERBOY IN TROUBLE

29 June 1969

Jamie looked at the telephone. He had a quick go at tidying his hair.

It rang again, impatiently, as though it thought that his hair was neither here nor there. So Jamie cleared his throat, picked up the receiver, made his voice as serious and shiny as possible, and said, "Hello?"

The voice on the other end was a woman's. She was muttering low and fast, so that Jamie had to jam the receiver against his ear to make sure he didn't miss anything. "Mr Finkleby?" (Helpfully, the Voice left no time for Jamie to confirm or deny this.) "I've got a scoop about Irena Dragunova you ain't gonna want to miss. Meet me at the stage door of the Angel Theatre in ten minutes."

"Um," began Jamie, "that won't be possi—"

But the Voice was not interested in what was or was not possi. "Ten minutes, Mr Finkleby! I'm about to go onstage, and then I'm leaving New York. I'm getting a bus out of here to Ohio. You meet me at the stage door in ten!"

And with that, the Voice hung up.

Jamie's mind was racing at double speed, so he put the receiver down extra slowly, to balance himself out. Bud was relying on him. He had to make sure this scoop wasn't lost. But Jamie had no idea where Bud was.

That only left him with one option. And it was an option that he liked.

Ten minutes – he would have to be quick. He pushed his swivel chair back hastily, lost control and crashed into the desk behind. Then he picked up Bud's Dictaphone and notepad and pen, put them in the pocket of his shorts, and hurried to the door.

The elevator was busy, so he ran down the spiralling

44

stairs, whirling and whirling round the great candle, picking up speed with each spin and flying out into the reception so fast that he didn't see Eve there until he crashed right into her and fell backwards on to the floor.

She blinked in surprise, and swayed down at him. "Oh! Are you all right? Sorry!"

"It wasn't your fault," said Jamie, standing up and brushing himself off.

"Ah," said Eve, "wasn't it? Well, that's a nice change. Where are you running to?"

"Got to meet my mother," said Jamie. The lie was automatic. It was partly because Bud had told him not to tell anyone, but it was mostly because he needed to get going, and the truth was bound to lead to a whole load more questions. He liked Eve, but other people slowed him down, and there wasn't time.

"Ah. I have to meet my grandfather," said Eve. "Mother is making me go with him to some tremendously dullsville gala show at the Angel."

Jamie stared. Of *course* she would be going to the same place. This was so annoying that he just kept staring and forgot about replying.

"Well," said Eve, "I guess I had better go and find her."

"Mmm."

"It was nice to meet you."

"Mmmm."

Eve looked at him for a moment longer, as though she was trying to take him apart and work out what made him tick. Then she shrugged a very slight shrug and drifted away across reception. The candlelight behind her was low by now, so she was led out by a very long shadow girl, with uneven curls.

Jamie gave her a three-minute head start, which felt like the longest three minutes that had ever happened in the history of mankind and possibly also dinosaurkind; then he *fwmph*ed out of the door, grabbed his bicycle and cycled the four blocks to the Angel Theatre.

The Angel was on Broadway. Here there were dense crowds of people, and the heat was overpowering, and all the buildings were riddled with neon lettering and rashes of flashing bulbs. Signs and posters shouted from every wall: the Angel was no exception. One poster screeched:

And another yelled:

A man was pasting a big red sticker saying CANCELLED over that one. And then, on a plain wooden door set into an alcove, there were two words picked out in black:

STAGE DOOR

Jamie chained up his bicycle, approached the stage door, turned on the Dictaphone, and knocked.

For a moment there was no reply. Then the door opened, and a woman's voice hissed, "Mr Finkleby?"

"Mm," said Jamie, vaguely.

"You listening, Mr Finkleby?"

"Mmm-hmmm."

"You got a notepad or something? You ready? I'm only going to say this once, d'you hear? I'm on stage any minute. You're alone, Mr Finkleby, you swear? Mr Finkleby? You're still there?"

"Still here," said Jamie, in his deepest voice. But maybe it wasn't deep enough, because the door opened a crack and two watery green eyes looked out. They narrowed.

"Hey, kid," said the Voice, "who are *you*?"

And before Jamie could decide whether and how to lie, three things happened very fast.

First, a shadow fell over him.

Second, the green eyes widened, then disappeared with a *bang* of the door.

Third, and most upsettingly, Jamie was circled by a strong arm, hoisted up and shoved into a car at an inconvenient upside-down angle.

By the time Jamie had righted himself, the man who owned the shadow and the strong arm was in the driver's seat. And Jamie had only got as far as saying "What—?" when they ran a red light, cut across the Broadway traffic and raced away down Forty-Third Street, leaving a trail of horn-honking and yelling in their wake.

After that, for a minute it was all Jamie could do to remember his own name and keep breathing. New York was sliding past at a sickening speed. It seemed to be lurching about, as the man weaved in and out of lanes and on and off the sidewalk with wild abandon. Jamie felt carsick and afraid-of-definitely-dying sick all at once. He banged on the window, and he yelled and yelled and yelled at the top of his considerable lungs.

It was no use. The city outside couldn't hear him,

and his fists bounced uselessly off the glass. As he yelled, the Beatles were singing on the radio that *All you need is love*, which was nice; but just then Jamie felt that what he *really* needed was something more solid, like a hammer, or a really good rock.

Apparently the driver didn't think much of the Beatles either, because he turned the radio off. To be more specific, he punched it repeatedly until it had stopped saying that *All you need is love* and started smoking slightly. So it was definitely off.

"How 'bout you shut it too, Mr Finkleby?" he suggested to Jamie. Jamie looked at the small crater where the radio used to be and nodded extra silently. "That's more like it," said the man. "Geez, you make some serious noise."

Jamie took his first proper look at his captor. He was enormous, and had to hunker down to fit inside the car. This produced a wrinkle between his bald head and his thick neck, which wriggled when he talked, like a limp lifeless mouth. In the rear-view mirror, Jamie could see that the man's real face looked much the same as his neck-face, with a matching mouth and two tiny eyes that barely punctured the desert of skin.

It didn't seem like the sort of face that you could reason with. But Jamie didn't have a lot of choice.

"Excuse me," he said, "I'm not actually Mr Finkleby."

"Suuure," said the man, rolling his tiny eyes, before punching his horn at a car in front that was foolishly driving at the speed limit. He overdid it a bit, and broke the horn.

"Seriously," said Jamie, "look at me. I'm twelve years old."

"Uh-huh." The man was staring stupidly at the hole where the horn used to be. Then he shrugged, wound down his window, and yelled, "HOOOOOOOOOOOONK" – which was surprisingly effective. The car in question let him pass. Starlings fled. A nearby skateboarder was so startled by the noise that she skated into a tree and dislodged a squirrel, which fell on a passing cyclist, who then couldn't see where he was going and wobbled right over into a bin.

The man wound the window up again, satisfied.

Jamie tried one more time. "Really, my name isn't Bud Finkleby. I'm not even a reporter. I'm a paperboy."

"Right," said the man, "and my name isn't Vinnie Costa, and I'm not even a hitman, I'm a mermaid." He chuckled at this idea, a low gurgle which made his wrinkle-smile wibble, before launching the car up on to the sidewalk to overtake an ambulance. "Anyways," he said, "even if I believed you – and I don't, because I'm not a *doofus* – you shouldn't have talked to that actress."

Jamie was starting to get used to the lurching motion of the car, and his brain was tentatively coming back to life. It began to sink in that Bud must have been on the trail of a seriously big scoop, if a killer had been sent to get him. And if Vinnie was going to insist, against all common sense, on treating Jamie like the *Yorker*'s top reporter – well, then, he might as well start acting like a top reporter. If he got out of this alive, he might just come away with The Idea, just like Pepe had predicted. It was a steadying thought; better than thinking about *not* getting out of it alive, anyway.

In his pocket, the Dictaphone was still on.

He had a feeling that Vinnie wasn't quite stupid enough to answer his questions outright. He had once read a library book about being a Top Reporter, and it said you should open people up during interviews by inviting them to talk about something they care about. Vinnie mostly seemed to care about punching things and driving like a lunatic.

"Say, Vinnie, there's a lot of lousy drivers out in New York today, huh?"

"Geez! Don't I know it! I swear there's no one in this city who can drive right, geez. I swear, on my mother's life" – and Vinnie couldn't punch his mother's life, so he punched the dashboard as a substitute.

"Sure. Must get tiring, all this traffic? Does your boss have you chasing around the city like this a lot?"

"Geez, every day ... GET OUTTA HERE!" he suggested to a nearby car. The car did not get outta there, mainly because it was, in fact, parked and empty.

"Every day? Don't you get weekends off? What's so urgent?"

Vinnie threw his hands up, to demonstrate general despair at his lot in life. Jamie couldn't decide if he felt less or more safe when Vinnie's hands were off the wheel. "Oh, everything, everything. My boss thinks every little thing's urgent. Vinnie, drive here, Vinnie, punch this, Vinnie, kill this guy, Vinnie, threaten to remove that guy's legs, blablablabla."

Jamie tried not to think too hard about these last two. "Sounds tough! How come there's so much to do?"

Vinnie didn't reply straight away, because he had to shout a series of short impatient honks out of the window while an old lady crossed the road. When that was over, he said, "Because my boss is an idiot, Mr Finkleby. Every job I'm asked to do, it just creates more problems. This month alone we already had trouble with this guy Art Johnson, who found out about the Arsonist, and now you're snooping around after that actress..." (Jamie was glad he had this all on tape, because he had a feeling this was probably a useful lead, if only his brain would stay still and think about it for a moment.)

"I dunno, Mr Finkleby," sighed Vinnie. "It seems to *me* like we could save a lot of trouble by just thinking things through with a bit more *smarts*." And he tapped himself on the head to show where smarts were kept, lightly concussed himself, swayed about for a few seconds, then took a sudden sharp left. "Well," he announced, "here we are."

They had stopped in a tunnel, dim and run-down and deserted. Nothing about it was even a little bit encouraging. Even though the car had stopped, Jamie started feeling sick again.

Vinnie got out of the car and came round to the passenger door, and Jamie got ready to make a run for it. But the moment Vinnie opened the door he scooped Jamie up in one enormous arm, one hand over his mouth, and it took all Jamie's strength just to wriggle about like a fish on a line. Vinnie might be stupid, but Jamie was horribly aware that right now, that didn't matter very much.

Still cradling Jamie, Vinnie squatted down and pulled up a manhole cover. Then he began to descend some steps, down into darkness.

Part of Jamie's brain registered that it was odd to find a flight of steps beneath a manhole cover. The rest of his brain was occupied by the bump, bump of his head on Vinnie's shoulder, and the chill that enveloped them as they made their way underground. Halfway down, Vinnie turned on a torch.

At the bottom of the stairs, he produced a length

of copper wire and tied Jamie to a pillar. He set the torch down beside him. Then he set to searching for something in his pockets – he was wearing grey overalls, which seemed to have endless pockets – while Jamie adjusted to being the right way up.

They were in a subway stop. Jamie was certain, even though he had his back to the tracks. It was unmistakable – the white-tiled walls streaked with yellow-brown stains, the cavernous concrete platform, the wooden benches, the silver newsstand. Through a green-tiled archway, he could see the gaping darkness of more archways, leading to more platforms.

It was a perfectly normal subway stop: except that it was entirely empty. It felt, somehow, as though it had been empty for a long time.

Vinnie had found his lighter in his pockets, and lit a cigarette. He had also found a trowel, some dog food, a soldering iron, a timer and some mittens, but none of this seemed to be what he was looking for.

"Geez," he sighed, turning the now-empty pockets inside out. "The stupid gun's still in the stupid car." He kicked a subway pillar. The clang reverberated.

Jamie had been scared before, but now all at once, he was blindly, blankly terrified. It hit him like a wave. It was hard to breathe.

"VinniepleaseIwillnevertell," he said, very fast. "I swear. I don't care about Irena Dragunova. I really don't. I'm not worth the effort."

"Mr Finkleby," sighed Bud, "if this was just about that actress, I would let you go. Geez. She's not important. This is about who *runs* this city. My boss is behind half the headline crimes of New York. It's all one big plan." He began wearily to reload his pockets. "If my boss was the measles of New York," he said, "Irena Dragunova would just be one unimportant scabby little spot." He paused for a moment at that, quite stunned by his own poetry, before continuing. "She's not important, I'm not important, you're not important. Geez, even right this minute, my boss is out in this city pulling off his latest trick. We're a sideshow." And he dragged heavily on his cigarette, and sighed.

Through the blank wall of fear, Jamie felt a twinge of resentment at this horrible timing. Clearly, whatever Vinnie's boss was up to, it would have won him Young

Reporter of the Year easily. He would have loved working out who this master criminal was, and what they were up to. And he was going to die before there was any time to investigate it.

"Wait there," said Vinnie – as though Jamie had any choice. And he went plodding back up the stairs, taking the torch with him. The only light left was the distant beam of a street light from above, which puddled at the bottom of the stairs.

So Jamie was left alone, with the enormous darkness. He could feel the Dictaphone still whirring gently in his pocket. He struggled against the wire.

Behind him there was a murmur, that grew to a rumble, that grew to an almighty roar. He felt a rush of wind as a subway train shot past behind him. Ten seconds later, with one last screech of metal on metal, it was gone.

That must have been why he didn't hear any footsteps. He didn't know that anyone else was there with him until he felt a tugging at the wire.

"Shh, don't yell, he might hear you. It's me." The tugging stopped, and the wire slipped away. Jamie turned.

"*Eve?*"

ESCAPE!

29 June 1969

Jamie sprang to his feet, whispering a fervent thank you. Eve stayed squatting and considered him, grey eyes wide, like a wise and gangly frog.

"You're not a very normal boy, are you?" she concluded. "What did you do to get yourself kidnapped?"

Jamie had questions of his own, but this didn't really seem like the time. "I'll explain," he said, starting for the stairs and the glorious light, "but let's get out of here first."

"OK," said Eve. She unfolded upwards. "Not that way,

though. The man's still out there." And she ambled off in the other direction, to the archways at the heart of the station.

"Eve! Where are you going?"

"I know another way out."

For a moment, Jamie hesitated. He didn't entirely trust her. But it was true that he had no plan to get past Vinnie, and Eve seemed utterly confident – and she *had* successfully snuck in to rescue him.

So he grabbed Vinnie's lighter from the pile of discarded belongings, flicked it on and followed his rescuer, further into the dark.

She led them to another platform. It was hard to see much with the lighter; it mostly just lit up itself, showing a fancy gold case with a flame embossed on the side. The platform flickered in and out of view with the trembling flame. Jamie couldn't see any exits, other than the way they had come in.

Eve sat down on the edge of the platform, legs dangling over the side. "Down here," she explained, pointing to the tracks.

Jamie was speechless. He was utterly without speech.

This was probably the worst idea in the history of terrible ideas.

"It's not live," Eve said. "This is a ghost stop. It's abandoned."

"The stop might be, but the tracks aren't," said Jamie. "A train came through earlier."

"On the other track, yes," said Eve patiently, "but not on this one. Trust me. We had to do a project on our favourite thing about New York for school, and I built a model of the subway system. I know it backwards." She looked up at him and waggled her dangling legs encouragingly. "It will be fine."

Based on the amount of effort *he* put into school projects, Jamie wasn't sure he trusted Eve's subway knowledge. But just then there was the heavy tramp of footsteps on stairs from the other platform: Vinnie. So Jamie hoped fervently that this was *actually* fine, and not fine in the way that lightly setting fire to yourself of a morning is fine, and he hastily put out his light and lowered himself alongside Eve on to the tracks.

It *seemed* to be fine.

There was no time for relief. There was a roar from the platform – Vinnie, discovering Jamie's absence – and without a word the children began to pick their way along the tracks towards the tunnel mouth.

The mouth gaped. The platform was dark, but the tunnel was somehow even darker.

They heard Vinnie's footsteps among the archways, but he tried a different platform first, off to the left. Jamie ran towards the tunnel; infuriatingly, Eve seemed content to plod. But it was difficult to run among the enormous sleepers in the gloom, and he kept falling, churning up his skin on the stones between the tracks. As he picked himself up for the sixth time, and Eve plodded through the tunnel mouth slightly ahead of him, he had to admit that there was something in her approach.

They made it inside the tunnel just seconds before Vinnie's footsteps arrived on their platform. Jamie slowed to Eve's pace, so that he could move among the metal and crunching stones quietly. He listened as they walked. Vinnie could be heard pacing and pausing, pacing and pausing, looking for him among the shadows; but the footsteps never dropped down on to the track. Jamie prayed that Vinnie didn't know which tracks were live.

Slowly, quietly, carefully, they left the sounds of Vinnie behind. Slowly, quietly, *carefully*, they kept moving forward through the endless, formless darkness. They were a long way from the platform, but Jamie had no idea how much further they had to go. He just had to hope Eve knew.

At this point there is no avoiding the awkward fact that Jamie Creeden was afraid of the dark. Or, more accurately, he was afraid of his own mind in the dark. Darkness seemed to him to be a special sort of emptiness, where all his worst thoughts suddenly had room to swell outwards, outwards and upwards, until they were huge and leering down at him.

Right now his worst thought was that he was going to die very soon in a subway tunnel, which is pretty bad as worst thoughts go; so when *that* swelled outwards, it was a bit overwhelming.

Something brushed against him, and he cried out slightly.

The something squeaked, and scuttled away indignantly.

"Just a rat, Jamie," said Eve kindly. (He was disconcerted to find that her voice now came from some way ahead.) "They don't hurt people."

They walked a little further.

"Unless they bite," she corrected herself, "and give you rat-bite fever."

They walked a little further.

"And they were kind of crucial for spreading the plague in Europe," she added, "so I guess they hurt people then. A lot of people. But, like, not directly."

"Eve, this isn't really helping."

"Sorry."

A little while later, Eve paused. Jamie could tell by the sudden silence. "What," he whispered, "what, what? What?"

"Oh, nothing," said Eve. "I'm just trying to remember which way we go here. It forks. I think it's *probably* left," she said— "Unless," she reasoned, "it's right."

Jamie thought he might actually be sick.

Just then there was a thunderous roar to their left,

very close by, with a regular *thud-thud*, *thud-thud*, and the anguished scream of metal on metal. It filled the whole tunnel. It filled the whole *world*. Jamie couldn't think straight.

"Ah," said Eve, when it had passed. "Right it is, then."

"Nggghhuh," said Jamie. It wasn't clear even to Jamie what that meant, except that it definitely wasn't "Oh great, that all seems fine". But he followed Eve to the right, because there was no other choice.

And a minute later there was a definite lighter patch ahead, and it grew and grew, until there was no room for doubt: it was the end of the tunnel. Even though he knew now that it wasn't useful, Jamie broke into a faltering-stumbling-knee-scraping run.

They heaved themselves up on the platform, and for a moment both just lay there in the gloom laughing hysterically, because it was over. The cool concrete beneath their backs felt wonderful. Their laughter echoed back to them.

The sound felt dangerously loud, and it brought them to their senses like a bucket of cold water. "Come on," said Eve, just as Jamie said, "We should go." So they clanged up the stairs, and emerged through another manhole cover at the fraying edge of downtown. Jamie breathed in the bright lights and the bustle, and smiled.

"Thank you," he said to Eve. Which wasn't enough, but it was difficult to know what else to say.

"Oh," she said. "No problem. We had better get out of here. He might figure out which way we went." And she wafted an arm at an approaching cab, which slowed at once. "Where do you need to go?"

"I left my bike at the Angel."

"Great. I have to meet Mother there when the show is over." So Eve asked the driver for the Angel Theatre, and for the second time that day Jamie found himself speeding through New York in a car.

It was infinitely better going at a sane speed. It was night now, and white globes of light had been turned on up and down the avenues, while every building was chequered with gold. Warm air buffeted their faces through an open car window. It was such a different world up here above ground that already Vinnie and that long dark tunnel began to feel like a dream. A really mad, carsickness-inducing dream.

"Right," said Eve. She had to yell a bit over the face-buffeting air. "Tell me everything."

"Um," said Jamie, glancing at the driver, "maybe when we're out of the cab."

"Ah yes, I see. All right."

There was an awkward little silence at that, so Jamie asked, "Will your mom be mad? That you didn't go with your grandfather to the gala, I mean?"

Eve shrugged. "A bit."

"Do you want me to explain? I mean, not explain *everything*, but say that you were helping me out? I could come up with a story."

"Oh, goodness no," said Eve. She wound up the passenger window, and the buffeting stopped. "That would make it worse. She'd hate you."

"Oh."

Eve did not seem to notice that she might have been a bit rude, or that a bit of her hair had got caught in the window. "My mother," said Eve, "has a plan for every minute of every hour of every day of my life. If I *always* did what she wanted, I would go mad. But if I never do it, she will send me off to a terrible boarding school

67

upstate which she says will teach me to be a lady. So I pick my battles."

She turned to Jamie, leaving the caught strands of hair behind, and looked as serious as she could manage given that there was some subway soot on her nose. "The trick is not to go mad. I protect myself by just tuning out. I have gotten very good at it. I go where she wants me to go, but in my *mind*, I go somewhere else." She tapped her head wisely.

"Right," said Jamie. The tapping went on, and he was a bit worried she might just keep tapping for ever if he didn't say something else. So he asked, "So missing the gala isn't a boarding school offence?"

"No. I went for my annual tour of Uncle Harry's, that was the main thing. I tried skipping that one year and she was *furious*."

"How come?"

"Oh, because she still hopes we will own the paper one day, and she always tells Grandfather lies about how keen I am on it all."

Jamie's face did acrobatics of wonderment and surprise at the revelation that Eve might actually be able to *own* the *Yorker*. He could not quite believe it. She sat there so calmly in her singed blue silk; if *he* was in her position, he didn't think he would ever be able to sit still, ever. He groped for the right question, and in the end settled for, "What?"

Eve shrugged, bored. "Grandfather still owns the paper. For now it's going to go to Uncle Harry when Grandfather dies, but every time sales are low, Grandfather threatens to give it to Mother. So Uncle Harry sells copies dirt cheap to keep sales high, and then he has to spend all his own money on the *Yorker* to stop it going bust like all the other papers."

"Wow!" said Jamie. To be honest, he had only really listened to the first bit. "You might own the paper? That's awesome!"

"Oh, not really. It just means that Mother and Uncle Harry hate each other, which is horrible."

"Oh," said Jamie.

Eve dipped her chin down into her hands and watched the bright lights slipping past. "The stupid thing is, neither of them actually *enjoy* newspapers, as far as I can tell. And they've got enough other businesses; they own half the city. They only want the *Yorker* because running a big newspaper makes you so powerful." She said "powerful" like it was the most tremendously boring thing you could possibly be. "Everyone wants to be nice to Uncle Harry, to make sure he prints good things about them. It's like he's royalty."

On balance Jamie thought this didn't sound like a very terrible situation. But he didn't press the point, because it seemed rude to argue with Eve when she had just saved his life. And by now the taxi had arrived among the neon flashes of Broadway once again, and was pulling up to the sidewalk.

Eve paid, and they stepped out into the crowds. Jamie felt giddy with happiness to be back in the warm air and bright lights of his own lovely city, crowded with the heat and noise of eight million other living, breathing people. He felt his own aliveness pumping through him, an answering call.

Eve checked her watch. "Ten more minutes of gala," she said. "Let's get hot dogs, and you can tell me everything."

So they did, and they ate them there and then by the

steaming stand, and it was the most wonderfully hot and salty and delicious thing Jamie had ever eaten or would ever eat, ever. Under the noise of the late-night traffic and chatter, he told Eve about Bud Finkleby's scoop, and the phone call, and the eyes behind the stage door, and Vinnie.

Eve listened with rapt attention, and didn't get distracted once. Then she told him how she had wandered into a record shop before going to the Angel, and arrived just in time to see him being shoved into the car. "I got straight into a taxi and told it to follow," she said. "It was brilliant. Like a movie." And she chuckled softly to herself. "I have *never* done anything like that before."

"Well, it was awesome."

"Yes," she said thoughtfully, "it was." She chewed the last of her hot dog, then said, "And what next?"

"Next?"

Eve shrugged. "Well, you aren't just going to let this go, are you?"

And now that Jamie was back under the bright Broadway lights again, he knew she was right. He wanted to be a reporter, and a reporter didn't give up a chance like this. This might have been Bud Finkleby's scoop once, but it was Jamie Creeden's scoop now.

"No," he said slowly, "I guess I'm not. I'm going to try and find out who Vinnie's boss is. Vinnie said they were behind half the crimes of New York, and it's all part of some master plan. If I can work out what they're up to…"

Eve nodded a satisfied nod, and licked salty grease off her fingers. Then she turned to look right at Jamie, with a look that was, startlingly, not at all vague.

"Can I help?" she said. "Mother actually doesn't have plans for me for the next week, for once. That only happens about once every three years." She saw him hesitating. "Please, Jamie. Tonight was brilliant. I never have any fun. I really want to help."

"OK," said Jamie. "Sure." He had always thought that other people slowed him down, but maybe Eve wouldn't. She *had* just saved his life. She seemed smart, and brave too – or at least, oblivious to danger, which came to the same thing.

So Eve gave him a card with her details, and Jamie

wrote his telephone number and address down on a spare *Eve Hooper-Banks* card; and they agreed to meet at her house the next morning, as soon as he could get there after his route.

As Jamie was writing, a trickle of people and laughter and elaborate hats began to flow from the Angel, and soon it was a full-scale flood: the gala was over. So the children said goodbye, and Eve drifted off, eyes dreamy once again, resolutely thinking herself somewhere else entirely.

Jamie was too exhausted to think straight. He put Eve's card in his pocket, unchained his bike, and forced himself to use one last burst of energy for the long cycle home: over the heavy darkness of the East River, down the shore of Brooklyn, down the steps to his own basement apartment.

It was all waiting for him, as though the evening had been nothing but a dream: the same old yellow kitchen, with the now-faded flower on the table; the same old bedroom with the newspaper-plastered walls and the boxes full of old *Yorkers;* the same old wonderful, glorious bed.

His mom was not yet home, as usual. For half a glorious second Jamie thought he would wait up for her at the kitchen table and unload everything to her, the whole wonderful-and-terrible day.

Then his brain intervened, and reminded him how upset and guilty she felt whenever anything bad happened to him. She wouldn't see this as an exciting opportunity: she would just be frightened. He could imagine her horrified, tearful face all too clearly. It made him upset just *thinking* about it. He would keep the events of today to himself, then, for now. He tried not to feel too bad about it. He could tell her *after* he had investigated, when it would be too late to worry and there would be no need for tears.

So he went to bed. Suddenly the exhaustion was overpowering. He curled right up under the covers without even pausing to change; and while life out in the city rolled on all through the night, Jamie Creeden slept soundly until dawn.

PAPERBOY ON THE TRAIL

30 June 1969

The next morning Jamie got up for his paper route in the dark as usual. But inside, he didn't feel at all usual. In fact, he was thoroughly distracted by the not-usualness of everything. It was exciting and terrifying in equal measure, and it made it impossible to sit still, or even to think a normal thought all the way through to the end without being distracted. He was so distracted that when he ate his breakfast he forgot to pour any milk on the cereal, and he cycled off to Lou's with his T-shirt on backwards.

He delivered the papers, but he hardly saw the dim streets that he cycled down: there was too much to think about. When his route was finished he almost forgot to pick a flower, and had to double back. He tried to write a note, but the enormity of everything he wasn't saying made him feel uncomfortable. In the end he just wrote *Yesterday was exciting – see you soon xxx*. Which still felt a bit like a lie, somehow, even though it wasn't.

For once, he didn't even stop to read the paper, and cycled right past the gossipers on the pier. He set straight out again, over to Manhattan. His first stop was the *Yorker*, to warn Bud that Vinnie might come looking for him. All the while, the sun crept up. By the time he was cycling over Brooklyn Bridge, the city spread before him was washed in early morning light, and the East River had turned a bright blue. It felt good to be back on his bike, doing what he did best. Everything would be all right, as long as he kept moving.

When he *fwmph*ed through the doors of the *Yorker*, the work day there had just begun: the candle clock was still magnificent at almost fifteen storeys tall.

The receptionist's boredom had ripened into

something powerful. She tried to ignore Jamie by pretending to be on the telephone, but he just put his elbows on the counter and waited, so in the end she had to unconvincingly pretend to hang up.

She told him that Mr Finkleby was not available.

"OK," said Jamie. "It's really important. Do you know when he'll be back?"

"He won't," she said. "He resigned this morning."

Jamie gawped at her. He had *resigned*?

"What? Why?"

She shrugged. "No idea. Goodbye," she said, with an especially firm sort of boredom, because she had no time for small boys with their T-shirts on backwards.

"Mm-hmm," said Jamie, lost in the whirligig of thoughts.

He *fwmphe*d back out of the *Yorker* offices into the heat outside, which by now had thickened into another sweltering day. For a moment he stood still in the shade of the tower, thinking. Bud had *resigned*? Had he already heard about the danger he was in, then? Jamie wished that he could have talked to him first; perhaps he knew something important.

Then he got back on his bike, and made for Eve's apartment.

Eve lived uptown, on Fifth Avenue. Manhattan is built on a grid system of long straight roads: numbered streets run the width of the island, and numbered avenues run the length. When you are at one end of an avenue, nothing blocks your view of the other end except the sheer distance. Yellow traffic lights are hung out against the sky like flags, and when one turns green, so do the others – green and green and green and green, all the way down.

Jamie sailed down Fifth Avenue, then slowed as he neared Eve's apartment, looking out for the numbers on the buildings he passed. Her building had a tunnel of dark red awning, with a dark-red-suited doorman at the end of it. The doorman was *very* polite, and helpfully did things like open the door and press the button on the elevator and delicately not mention Jamie's T-shirt.

Jamie reached apartment number four, and knocked.

He prepared his best polite-to-parents face, but it

was Eve herself who opened the door. She was in some old dungarees, her curls were tied back with an elastic band and there was some paint splattered on her face, so Jamie suspected that her mother wasn't home.

"Hello!" she said. Her head bobbed at him in a pleased sort-of greeting. "Got a lot on your mind?"

"Um," said Jamie, "yeah, actually. Is it that obvious?"

"Your T-shirt is on backwards."

"Ah." Jamie considered this, and decided it probably wasn't very important. "Yes. Lots on my mind. I reckon I've got some ideas."

"Great!" said Eve, "Well, come in" – and she stepped aside to let him pass.

Jamie tried to look like he saw apartments like this every day.

It was huge. The ceiling dripped chandeliers, and the floor was covered in a carpet so soft that even Jamie couldn't make a sound with his footsteps.

Everything, he realized as he looked around, was white-and-gold. Little chocolates in bowls were wrapped in white-and-gold, and books lining one wall were all identically bound in white-and-gold leather, and the vases full of white lilies had their stems painted gold. In an alcove, a terrifying white-and-gold replica of the *Yorker* statue glared at him, with her solid gold candle and her pearl hourglass held aloft.

A particularly fluffy patch of white-and-gold came shuffling up to them. It appeared to be a moving cushion.

"That's Pumpkin," said Eve, "the world's most tremendously useless dog. Mother bought him when it was fashionable to carry dogs in handbags, but he kept eating the bags, so now I'm stuck looking after him."

Pumpkin sniffed Jamie's leg, tried to shuffle off backwards and let out a *wurff* of surprise. He seemed to be stuck to Jamie's leg.

"Oh, not *again*, Pumpkin," said Eve. "Sorry about this. I've been building a model of Brooklyn Bridge, and he thinks the glue is some sort of doggy snack." She bent down and gave the dog a tug, which made Jamie say "Ow" and Pumpkin say "Owwrrff" but did the job.

"Bad dog," said Eve, not very convincingly. "Right, let's hear what you're thinking. Have a seat. I'll get us some lemonade." And Eve pointed Jamie to a living room the size of his whole apartment, then went off to get lemonade, Pumpkin trotting faithfully behind her.

Jamie perched on the edge of the white-and-gold sofa. From the wall opposite, twelve photos of Eve looked back at him, each one older than the last. The youngest ones were smiling; the middle ones began to scowl; and then by the end Eve had begun to adopt the dreamy, evasive gaze. In those last photos, she barely seemed to be there at all. The photos were surrounded by certificates, for clarinet exams and etiquette classes and dancing (which was difficult to imagine) and...

"Lemonade!" announced Eve. "Ah," she said, "I see you're admiring Mother's shrine to the daughter she wishes she had." She put down two glasses and curled up on the sofa. Pumpkin repeatedly tried to jump up into her lap, but he could only get about an inch off the floor. "I think she's still hoping that if she sends me on the right course, I'll wake up all sophisticated and cultured and ready to make sparkling conversation at cocktail parties."

Jamie looked from the frozen, absent Eves back

to the happy, paint-splattered Eve on the sofa. He felt a little sorry for her. But right now she was waiting eagerly for news, and they had a job to do. "So," he said, "shall I fill you in on what I know so far?"

Eve nodded eagerly, and her curls bobbed into her lemonade. She finally noticed Pumpkin, and scooped him up into her lap, where he happily slurped the lemonade from her hair.

Meanwhile, Jamie was taking *Yorker*s from his satchel. "So. Vinnie says his boss is behind half the headline crimes in New York, and they all add up to some kind of master plan. I want to know who this boss is, and what they're up to. So far, I know about two headlines that they were responsible for. The disappearing actress is one, obviously. Did you read about her? Irena Dragunova?"

Eve shook her head. "I never read the news. Mother leaves a *Yorker* on my bed every morning, but I have been turning them into a papier mâché model of the Saturn V rocket to make a point."

"Oh," said Jamie, "cool." He spread out the front page from the day he'd first met Harry Hooper, four days ago. "Well, take a look." And he reread, while Eve read:

Thursday June 26 1969

No 40735

MORNING
YORKER 10¢

IRENA DRAGUNOVA VANISHED!

By BUD FINKLEBY

Irena Dragunova, much-loved star of the Russian stage, vanished mysteriously from the Angel Theatre last night, just hours after arriving in New York City from the USSR. She was intending to perform her one-woman show at the Angel for a hotly anticipated two-month run, which had sold out despite the record high price of tickets.

Miss Dragunova arrived at the theatre at 6:40, surrounded by her personal security guards, and entered her dressing room. One hour later, when she was called onstage, it was discovered that the dressing room was empty. The theatre searched high and low, but two hours later they were forced to announce her disappearance, and turn the disappointed audience away.

Police are stumped, according to Detective Da Costa. "It's a real puzzler. She had brought six security guards, and they were outside the door the whole time. That dressing room has three tiny high-up windows, you couldn't get a cat through them. The walls were, y'know, walls – solid and all."

Miss Dragunova was one of the very few citizens of the USSR permitted to travel to the USA this year. Tensions between the two states run as high as ever, and travel is still restricted to selected artists and performers. Police are appealing for any information, ideas, or general words of encouragement to help with their enquiries.

"So," said Jamie, "we don't know if she was kidnapped, or escaping something, or what. But we know she vanished. And that brings me to the second case." He spread out another front page.

"Vinnie said that he had trouble with some guy called Art Johnson, because he found out too much about ... the Arsonist." Dramatic pause. No reaction. "You *must* have heard of the Arsonist! There've been more headlines about him than any other criminal in New York! I've got them all in my bag; this one's jus t the latest, it's from yesterday."

Eve restrained Pumpkin from eating the page, and leaned forward to look.

"So," Jamie went on, "if Vinnie's boss is behind the arson attacks *and* the disappearing actress, then we need to know what connects them. So far, all I can see is that he's another vanishing act."

So they read:

MORNING
YORKER 10¢

ARSONIST STRIKES ON UPPER EAST SIDE

By BUD FINKLEBY

The Arsonist struck again last night, starting a fire which entirely destroyed the Carnation Building on Madison Avenue.

The attack followed a now-familiar pattern. The blaze was first reported at 8:45 p.m. As the flames consumed the building, the Arsonist remained inside. Using a megaphone, he thanked the crowds for coming, before playing them a haunting concert on his violin. The playing reportedly lasted for about an hour. Then, sometime before the fire was quelled, the man made his escape unseen through the flames, past the firefighters and the crowd of onlookers that surrounded the building.

"It's quite impressive," remarked Davey Hale, Fire Commissioner of the New York City Fire Department. "But it's also really, really, really, really, really, really annoying."

We asked the mayor of New York whether he thought the time had come for tougher action on the Arsonist. "Yes, yes," he remarked, toughly. And he looked really fierce while he said it, so it is the opinion of this reporter that he meant business.

But for now, the Arsonist remains at large, and New York can only wait in fear and awe for him to return. Where will he strike next?

BLAST OFF!
Inside this issue:
the latest on the
Apollo lunar
mission.

Eve spoke first. "Well," she said, "I have no idea where to start. It makes me feel fuzzy just trying to think about it. Why would someone vanish an actress and burn down a load of buildings? Where do you even *begin*?"

"Reporters are meant to ask themselves *what, when, where, who, why, how*," recited Jamie. He had read this in his Top Reporter book. "We know what, when and where. I'm going to start with the *who* and *why*. I've got one lead: last night, Vinnie said they had trouble because Art Johnson knew something about the Arsonist. So I'll start by calling all the *JOHNSON, As*, in the phone book, and if I find Art, I'll try and get him to talk to me. While I'm doing that," he went on, "I thought you could work on the *how*. If you want." He leaned forward. "That actress vanished from her dressing room, which was guarded from the outside. The only windows were too small for her to fit through. So – how?"

He had guessed right: the puzzle suited Eve. She jumped up at once and ran to the bookshelves, returning with the phone book for Jamie and a heavy hardback tome entitled *Architecture of New York: 1900–1960*.

"Architectural plans," she said, "for all the major

buildings in New York – including the Angel. There might be a clue in here." She settled back on to the sofa. "There will be a way out, we've just got to find it – people don't disappear."

Jamie nodded, impressed. Eve might *seem* a bit vague, but she got things done.

"By the way," she said, "Uncle Harry owns the Angel Theatre, so you might want to try talking to him, too."

Jamie logged that detail for later. Interesting that Harry Hooper had a connection to the theatre. So far, he didn't know anybody else connected to the actress.

Then Eve began calculating which walls might be thick enough for a hidden passage and where a trapdoor could be inserted and what the odds were of surviving a jump from the windows, while Jamie opened the phone book at *JOHNSON, A*. There were a *lot* of *JOHNSON, As*. Jamie thought of the weary researchers at the *Yorker*. He wondered whether he ought to learn to like coffee.

There was nothing to do but begin. He spoke to Adam Johnson and Amy Johnson and Albert Johnson and Alice Johnson. Andy Johnson tried to sell him a second-hand car. Ashley Johnson told him that aliens were secretly running New York from their base on Venus. Agnes Johnson told him that her parrot had the flu.

"Cheer up," said Eve, after he hung up on Abraham Johnson, who introduced him to each of his kittens over the phone one by one. "You'll get there."

"Any luck with the theatre?"

Eve frowned at a sheet of paper she had been covering in sums. "Nope. She couldn't have fit through a window, they're definitely much too small. The walls aren't thick enough for secret passages or hidden rooms. Any trapdoor from her floor would lead right through to the auditorium below, which would have been staffed the whole time. I can't work it out. She *had* to leave by the door." She picked up the paper again. "And if she used the door, it must all be in the timing, somehow…"

Eve returned to her sums. Jamie sighed, picked up the phone again and tried yet another *JOHNSON, A.*

"Hello?" The person who picked up was female, and sounded young.

"Hi," said Jamie. "Does Art Johnson live here?"

"Yes. But he's not here right now. This is Rose."

Jamie spilt lemonade on top of Pumpkin in his excitement. Pumpkin couldn't work out whether this was a good thing or a bad thing, and did a little circular trot of confusion.

"Hello, Rose," said Jamie. "This might seem like an odd question, but – does the Arsonist mean anything to you?"

There was a long silence before Rose replied. "Who is this?"

"My name's Jamie Creeden," said Jamie, "And I'm working for the *Morning Yorker.*" (He didn't think of this as a lie, exactly. He had every intention of seeing his name in print.)

"The press?" Rose sounded alarmed.

"We're on your side, Rose!" said Jamie hastily. "We believe someone has been giving Art trouble. A big bald guy called Vinnie? I want to know who he's working for, and what they're up to. We're hoping Art can help."

There was another long silence. Rose was breathing very quickly on the other end.

"Rose?"

"I'll meet you and hear you out," she said finally. "Tonight, six o'clock?"

"Great! Yes! Great!" said Jamie, and he scribbled down the address she gave.

"The password is *lilliput*," she said.

"What? Why do I need a password?"

But Rose had hung up.

Jamie turned to Eve, who was waiting expectantly, and told her the plan.

"Great," she said, smiling a rare smile, "let's—"

But just then there was the sound of a key in the lock, and her smile slithered off again.

"Ugh. She's early," she whispered. Then she quickly arranged her face into the dreamy, innocent look Jamie had seen at the *Yorker*.

Eve's mother was home.

ART
JOHNSON'S DAUGHTER

30 June 1969

Pearl Hooper-Banks was as white-and-gold as her apartment. She a gold helmet of hair, and a crisp white summer dress. Her hair curled like Eve's, but hers had been persuaded to cluster neatly around her skull; and she had Eve's grey eyes, but hers were cold and unforgiving.

"Hello," she said, "who's this?" Her voice was refined, and sharp at the edges. Her eyes raked Jamie up and down.

"Hello," said Jamie, "I'm Jamie." And he recited politely, "It's-a-pleasure-to-meet-you-and-you-have-a-lovely-home."

"A pleasure indeed," said Pearl. "Eve so rarely has friends over. She didn't mention you were coming, dear."

"It was a last-minute plan, Mother," said Eve calmly.

"I see." Pearl's eyes continued to size Jamie up. "How did you two meet?"

"Um." Jamie thought quickly. Clearly Eve hadn't mentioned meeting him at the Yorker, and he didn't know what story she had come up with about last night. "School," he said, to be safe.

Pearl raised her eyebrows. "At ... St Philomena's School for Girls?"

"He's at St Mark's," said Eve quickly. "But he's in the orchestra. You remember the orchestra is for both schools, Mother," she added, for Jamie's benefit.

"Lovely," said Pearl. "Speaking of which, Eve, we're late – I've booked you in for an extra clarinet lesson. Get your things."

There was a brief moment of rebellion in Eve's eyes.

Then she smothered it under an extra-thick layer of vagueness, and drifted off to her bedroom.

Jamie, Pearl and Pumpkin waited. Pearl just stood quite still, looking at Jamie, and not speaking. She gave Jamie the creeps. Pumpkin didn't like the atmosphere, and chewed nervously on his own ear.

About a minute into the silence, Jamie remembered that his T-shirt was still on backwards.

When Eve returned at last, she had her clarinet, a satchel and a piece of paper. "Here are the details of the concerto recording I was telling you about," she said, handing Jamie the paper. "The second movement's tremendous."

Jamie unfolded the paper:

Meet at 86th and 5th, 5:30

"Great," he said, doing what he hoped was a pleased-about-concertos face while giving her the ghost of a wink. "I'll check it out."

"Goodbye, dear," said Pearl. She walked out into the hallway and opened the front door. Jamie followed and stepped outside.

"Bye," he said. "Bye, Eve."

She bobbed her head in farewell, and Pearl firmly shut the door in his face.

When he was back outside, Jamie got on his bike, where he did his best thinking. He headed for Central Park to cycle round and round the paths and think round and round everything he knew. He still couldn't see what an actress and an arsonist had in common, and why they would be so important. Vinnie had said that it was all about *who runs this city*, but Jamie couldn't see how.

He cycled past a stall selling crushed ice, and paused, feeling in his pocket for change. He counted out everything he had, including Vinnie's lighter and some tissues, but it wasn't quite enough. He wondered if he could barter the lighter, which seemed pretty posh. From the weight, it might even have been gold, and the hourglass engraving was beautiful.

As he was putting it back in his pocket, it occurred to him that the engraving had changed. Hadn't it been a flame before?

He took it back out. There *was* a flame, on the other side. A flame for truth, and an hourglass for punctuality.

Jamie forgot all about crushed ice. What was Vinnie doing with an expensive *Yorker*-crested lighter?

He carried on forgetting the crushed ice, and forgot to breathe as well. He knew exactly who might be able to give him such a lighter. Someone who owned the very theatre where the actress had gone missing, and could go backstage there any time he liked. Someone who could *definitely* be described as *running this city*, because he controlled the news, and his paper was so powerful that everybody from the president down wanted to take him for lunch.

Jamie put the lighter slowly back in his pocket. He still had no idea *why* Harry Hooper would want to kidnap an actress or burn down buildings. And he knew it was a bad idea to dwell too much on hunches, before you had all the facts. But Harry would make such a deliciously sensational villain. It was hard *not* to dwell on it.

Still, he thought it might be best not to mention it to Eve just yet. He *was* her uncle, after all.

He met her again at 5.30, at the corner where

Eighty-Sixth Street and Fifth Avenue met, to go and see Rose Johnson. Eve had a very beautiful bicycle, with a basket that was just the right size for Pumpkin, if he sort-of squashed in his nose a bit.

"Hi, Eve," said Jamie, "Hi, Pumpkin."

"Hi," said Eve.

"Wrf," said Pumpkin, in a sort-of-squashed-in-a-bit way.

"Ready?"

"Ready."

So they set off uptown to Harlem.

The cycle ride was hot and noisy, but Rose's street was a pleasant relief; the trees met in an arch over the road and cast everything into a dappled shade, people lounged on the stoops outside their houses, and the lazy chatter of evenings drifted from open windows. They free-wheeled peacefully down to her house, at the far end.

When they got there, they braked their bikes and looked at each other. The house was a lot less nice. Windows were broken and patched up. The white paint peeled like old skin, showing the fleshy red underneath, and one of the two stone lions guarding the stoop was missing its head.

Leaving the bikes, they approached the stoop and looked at the line of doorbells. The JOHNSON bell, like a lot of the others, looked broken. But a note taped under it said *R Johnson is in the yard*, with an arrow, which pointed to an overgrown strip of grass at the side of the house. The yard was behind a wire mesh fence, with half a sign that said "Trespassers will be". There was no obvious gate, but a gap had been torn in the bottom of the wire.

"Right," said Jamie. And there was nothing to do but crawl through it; so they did, Eve manoeuvring awkwardly with Pumpkin in her arms.

Jamie made it through unharmed, but there was not quite enough room for Eve's great height, and she came through with a scrape on her forehead for her troubles.

"Ooh, that looks bad. You all right?"

"Fine, fine."

They approached the tent.

"Um," called Jamie, suddenly feeling a bit foolish.

"Hello?"

From inside, a girl's voice called, "Password?"

Jamie opened his mouth, then stopped. He knew that a password had been mentioned on the phone, but he couldn't remember for the life of him what it was. "Er," he said, "lollypuck?"

A face came out from among the blankets. It was heart-shaped, and young, perhaps a little younger than Jamie – although it wore such a serious expression that it looked strangely old. Big eyes blinked behind big round spectacles. Rose Johnson looked like an especially grave sort of owl. And she appeared to be wearing a firefighter's helmet.

"Nope," she began, "but close…" Then she saw Eve's forehead. "Oh," she gasped, "you're hurt! Come in, come in." And the fabric parted, admitting Jamie and Eve into the tree-trunk den of Rose Johnson.

It was cool and shady inside. The sounds of the city faded as the blankets swung shut. It felt like they were somewhere else entirely now – as though somebody had carved a slice out of the sweltering day and tucked this place inside it. The tree's trunk and several of its branches were inside the den, and candles hung from them in colourful glass globes. Overhead, two squirrels watched them, noses quivering, tails held aloft.

"Wow," said Eve softly.

Rose, meanwhile, had produced plasters and cream from one of the many baskets hanging from the branches, and a bottle of water from a crate on the floor. She sat on one of the old rugs and cushions that had been piled around the old stump of another tree, and gestured for Eve and Jamie to sit too. "Brother," she said, "it looks bad. Hold tight, this might sting." And she tipped her helmet back to see better, and carefully mopped up Eve's forehead with her right hand, holding back the ever-unhelpful curls with her left.

"Thanks," said Eve.

"I'm really sorry," said Rose, "I keep meaning to do something about that fence."

"It's not a big deal," said Eve. "I injure myself all the time. Mother gets tremendously upset."

Rose apparently missed the bitter scorn in Eve's voice. She took this upset mother *very* seriously, and her wide eyes widened even further. "Oh, poor lady," she said.

"Oh, no, not really," said Eve. "She gets upset about every tiny thing. It's stupid."

"*Oh*," said Rose. The idea of somebody who was upset by *everything* was too much for her to bear; her eyes shone with sympathetic tears. She smoothed the plaster down very carefully. "I'm sorry. That must be very hard for her. And for you. Oh brother."

"Um," said Eve.

Rose set three cracked old teacups with mismatched saucers on the tree stump; she poured out water into each of them, and put three sticks of bubblegum on the plates. "I hope it wasn't too far for you to come," she said as she handed out the cups. "I'm not meant to talk about my dad and the – the you-know-who – but he's so sad about it all that I have to try and do *something*. But I had to meet you first, and make sure I could trust you." She drew her knees in to her chest, and looked at them over her teacup. "You're not what I was expecting."

Which was a bold thing for a small girl in a firefighter's helmet hosting a bubblegum tea party in a tree-based wonder tent to say. Jamie did not think he was the most

100

surprising person there, by quite a long way.

He started a question, but Rose shook her head. "You first," she said. "You have to tell me who you are, and why you want to know about all this."

Jamie hesitated, unsure of how much to share. He looked at Eve for support, but Eve was blowing a bubble with avid fascination; from the look of delight in her eyes, Jamie guessed she had never been allowed bubblegum before. He was on his own.

"Well," he said, "it's like this."

And he ended up telling Rose everything. She looked at him so intensely that he felt she would see if he missed anything out. And she was a good audience, gasping and sighing in all the right places, and asking lots of interested questions, and even shedding tears for the poor vanished actress and all the imagined people who might have loved her.

This whole time, Eve sustained one enormous bubble. She had a natural talent for it. It finally popped, loudly, in the silence that followed Jamie's speech.

"And Eve," added Jamie, "is, er, also here. She's …" He searched for the right phrase to explain Eve, and

Harry Hooper came to mind. ". . . very brilliant."

Rose nodded, as if this was very evident and absolutely fine, while Eve peeled some stray gum off her nose and smiled a hello.

"OK," said Rose. Her solemn eyes had widened to maximum solemnity, and they shone in the candlelight. "I'm going to tell you my dad's story. But there's two conditions. First, don't ever try and interview my dad. You'll only upset him. He's really fragile right now." The others nodded. "Second, you have to let me help you. I want to know the truth, too. I've *got* to."

Jamie hesitated. He hadn't planned on *one* person joining him, let alone two; but he needed Rose's story. "OK," he said, "sure."

"All right, then," said Rose. "You should both shut your eyes." They looked at her. "It's easier to imagine stories when you shut your eyes," she explained.

So they did. At first Eve and Jamie spent ages doing that thing where you sneak peeks at each other through half-shut eyes to make sure the other person is also definitely shutting their eyes, but eventually they got the hang of it and settled back on their cushions. Then, and only then, Rose Johnson told the story of Art Johnson and the Arsonist.

"My father is a firefighter," she began. "A really good firefighter. The best. And sometimes he let me go along to his shifts at the firehouse. He's not really meant to, but everybody there likes us so it's fine. You have to imagine this big warehouse full of men in uniform, and rows of these huge silent engines, and everybody just waiting around and playing cards. You imagining?"

(They were. I hope you are.)

"Now, every night this year they'd been wondering if they might get called out for the Arsonist. And this one night a few weeks ago he finally strikes in our unit's district, at the Juniper Building in Midtown. And this time, oh *brother*, it was the biggest fire I've ever seen. And I've seen fires. You need to imagine this whirl of heat and light and smoke so angry and loud it's like it's alive. You won't be able to imagine the smell 'cause smells are hard, but you can think what it looked like. And there's a huge crowd watching, and the Arsonist playing this spine-tingling music, and everyone's battling really hard to get the fire back under control.

But it's fighting back. I've never seen a fire like it: it was *alive*."

Jamie felt his skin crawl. It was surprisingly crawly, in fact. He opened his eyes to double check, and found that the feeling was actually the tail of a squirrel, shivering against his leg. He shut his eyes again.

"So my dad and two others, Sam and Pedro, get sent up on ladders to where the Arsonist is. And only Sam and Pedro come out." Rose took a deep breath. "They said Dad had gotten through to the room where the Arsonist was, but then the wall collapsed and they couldn't get in after him. There were a few awful minutes, and then my dad comes back out."

Rose took another shaky breath. Pumpkin sneezed, and Eve *sh*-ed him.

"So his face is all staring," Rose went on, "and the violin is playing and playing. We wrap him in a blanket and I run over the road for some sweet tea, for the shock. When I come back, there's some really tall bald guy talking to him."

"Vinnie!" said Jamie, opening his eyes.

"I guess," said Rose. "He's big, and mean-looking.

I'm not close enough to hear what he's saying, but he sees me and points at me and says something to Dad, and Dad stands up and starts shouting. Then he goes away again."

"What was he saying?" said Jamie. "Did your dad tell you?"

"Nope," said Rose, huddling further into her knees. "But I reckon it was a threat." And Jamie reckoned she was right. "The next day," she went on, "he quits his job. That bald man must've made him do it. He *loved* his job. And he can't get another one because all he knows how to do is fight fires, so we're in trouble. We've been kicked out of our old apartment already – that's why we're in there." She jerked her head in the direction of the peeling apartment block outside.

Neither of the others knew what to say to that.

"He's going to be a firefighter again, I just know it," said Rose. She pointed to her helmeted-head, and added, "I'm going to be one too, one day. The others in his company gave me this for my birthday."

And they *really* didn't know what to say to that, because it was difficult to imagine a more unlikely firefighter than Rose Johnson. But Jamie remembered Bud Finkleby laughing at them both by the printing press, and didn't say a word.

Meanwhile, Rose reached under a cushion and pulled out a small wooden box. Using a key on a ribbon round her neck, she opened it and took out a stack of letters. "Dad's been getting these threatening notes," she said. "And the bald guy comes round our house sometimes, and this week there's been this woman with blonde hair too. They must be posting the notes, I guess."

"A blonde woman?" said Jamie, thoughtfully. Was that Vinnie's boss? "Who's that?"

"No idea," said Rose. "Our apartment's on the top floor so I just see the top of her head." She sighed and hugged her knees. "I guess I'm not much of a detective. Oh brother, I wish I could help him, but I just can't make anything of it. What about the letters? Are they any use?"

Jamie looked through them, while Rose watched him with big, hopeful eyes. The notes were made of old cut-up newspapers, so that you couldn't trace the handwriting, and most were just nasty threats, dubiously spelled.

"We got one more today," said Rose, handing him a final note from her pocket:

NOONE BELEIVES JOSEPH WOOLF AND NOW HES IN BIG tRUBLe. THATS WHAT hAPeNs to PEEPLe who TALK.

KEEP YOUR MOUth ShUT

Jamie studied it. "Who's Joseph Woolf?" he asked.

Rose's eyes widened. "Haven't you heard?" But the others obviously *hadn't* heard, so she explained, "*Everybody's* talking about it. He was all over the papers this morning."

"Oh," said Jamie, "er. I didn't actually read the paper this morning." He blushed. Inside, he was kicking himself. It was the first time in five years that he had gone without reading it, and he had missed something important.

He reached for his satchel and pulled out his unread *Yorker*; sharing with Eve, they both read.

When they had finished, there was a short silence.

Eventually, Eve said, "Well then," quietly.

"Yes," agreed Jamie, looking at the face that scowled up at him from the page. Joseph Woolf did *not* sound like somebody he particularly wanted to meet.

But he had to. Woolf was the next lead. He chewed his gum, and tried to look braver than he felt.

"So. Right. Do either of you know," he said, "how we can visit someone in Long Island Jail?"

NIGHT-TIME

30 June 1969

By the time Jamie arrived back in Bay Ridge, the shortened *Goodnight, New York* was already finishing: Cindy Bell wished New York her trademark goodnight, and the new reporter began their piece on a hot-dog-eating competition. Pepe said he hadn't missed much – "Nothing that wasn't in the paper. Her days as New York's finest reporter are over, my friend" – and made Jamie a quick chocolate milkshake before shutting for the night.

When he arrived home, there was a note from his mom on the table:

Hello, pet! That was a short note! Is everything all right? I want to hear all about the Yorker! Did you have fun? I'm starting late tomorrow morning, so maybe I'll see you after your route and you can tell me all about it?
Love you xxx

Underneath the note was a pile of letters in brown envelopes. They were the sort of letter that made his mom sigh and look more worried than ever. And next to *those* was a plain white envelope, addressed to JAMIE CREDEN.

Jamie's gut curled inwards sharply. It wasn't, somehow, a friendly sort of envelope. And the bad spelling was horribly familiar.

He picked it up, opened it, and read the note inside:

GOT THE WRONG GUY
THE OTHER DAY - SORY
KEEP QUIET IF YOU
DONT WANT TRUBLE

Jamie read it. He read it again. He shut his eyes and opened them, but it was still there.

Vinnie had been here. Inside Jamie's apartment. He knew his name. He knew where he lived.

Jamie was used to the drab silence of his apartment, but suddenly, he couldn't stand it. It seemed alive with tiny draughts that might be breaths, and faint creaks that might be footsteps.

He read the note one more time. He went round the small apartment turning on every light and propping open every door, including all the cupboards, until there was nowhere left hidden: and *that* felt better.

But then something thudded gently just outside the front door.

He spent an awful minute frozen, listening. But nothing happened.

In the end he ran to the front door and wrenched it open. He rushed up the steps and looked left, and right, and left again. Nothing. It was just a normal, unimportant thud. He took an enormously deep breath and turned his face upwards, to the sky.

There were not a lot of stars to see, because of all the light pollution. When Jamie was small and had first learned what stars were, he had wished that he lived somewhere where you could see them. Then his mom pointed out that for every star that he couldn't see, a light was on somewhere in New York City: a street light, or a bright living room lamp, or the beam of a ship between the islands, or the headlights of a car. "In this city," she had told him, "we keep our stars on the ground. We make our fate down here, not up there."

Ever since then, the empty faded-black of the night sky made Jamie think of eight million people with their lights on, and he liked it better than stars. But tonight, it wasn't as comforting as usual. How had Vinnie found *him*, out of all those eight million?

A breeze had picked up. A soda can and a paper bag waltzed past in a forlorn duet. Jamie watched them, and thought to himself that maybe he should do what Vinnie said. He should just keep quiet and write his neighbour's idea about the trash collection, and forget about it all.

But if he did that, then he wouldn't have a hope of winning the Young Reporter. And it certainly wouldn't help Art and Rose and the missing actress.

And anyway: he didn't *want* to write about trash. And he didn't want to keep quiet. He was a reporter, and a good one.

He went back inside.

He unpinned the articles from the wall over his bed, until he had cleared a large square. Then he pinned up every article he had about the actress and the Arsonist. Underneath these, defiantly, he pinned Vinnie's note.

Then he settled down to reread the day's headline on Joseph Woolf. He got into bed and pulled the covers right up to his chin, despite the warm night. Every creak still made his guts squeeze, but he did his best to ignore them. He read out loud, just to break the silence:

Monday June 30 1969

No 40739

MORNING

YORKER 10¢

ASSASSIN ATTACKS MAYOR WILSON

By Bud Finkleby

An assassin fired at the much-loved, popular and handsome mayor of New York last night, as he was having drinks in a private room at the Pellier Club with the Yorker's own Harry Hooper. The shot missed, and the mayor is unharmed. A security guard has been arrested for the crime, but protests his innocence.

The shaken mayor explained that the bullet had come through the room's open window. It was fired from the Manhattan Downtown Public Library, which is opposite the Pellier Club across a narrow alley. The last visitors to the library left when it shut at 6:00 p.m., and an electrician left the site at 7:30 p.m.; when shots were fired two hours later, the only person present in the building was the building's security guard, Mr Joseph Woolf.

The gun was found in a room on the sixth floor. Mr Woolf was also on the sixth floor. He saw nobody else there, but protests that he is innocent.

"It wasn't me. No, I don't know who it was. No, I don't know how they could've gotten away. They couldn't. Any more stupid questions?" said Mr Woolf, in a statement which police described as "not especially useful".

Mayor Wilson was visibly shaken, but noble and brave as ever, taking time to thank the police at the scene, make friends with a poor child and pet a puppy. He is standing for mayor again this summer. One witness at the scene commented, "Gee, what a great guy. He sure has my vote. Wowzer."

Mr Woolf remains in custody at Long Island Jail, awaiting trial and no doubt thinking evil thoughts.

Jamie folded the paper up thoughtfully. Joseph Woolf glared at him from underneath the headline, teeth slightly bared, looking every inch the villain. If Woolf was telling the truth, then who had fired the shots, and how had they escaped? Just like the Arsonist and the actress, the true assassin had vanished into thin air. How?

And *who*? Jamie was back to square one on that question. Vinnie had told him, last night in the subway stop, that as they spoke, his boss was pulling off another of his crimes. This botched assassination must have been what he meant. Which, annoyingly, ruled out Harry Hooper: he was in the room with the mayor at the time, so he couldn't have been the mystery shooter. But who else might have given Vinnie that *Yorker*-crested lighter?

The three cases went round and round in his head. The actress. The Arsonist. The assassin. What did they all have in common? How did they fit into the master plan that Vinnie had talked about? Rose had seen a blonde woman: was *she* the mysterious boss?

He puzzled over it all for a long time. He might

have gone on puzzling all night, but he realized that his mom was due home in ten minutes or so, and he absolutely couldn't tell her about the threatening notes. She would be much too upset. He had to fix this first. So he took down Vinnie's note and turned out the light in his room – but he left on all the others, just to be safe.

He couldn't sleep. He only really rested once he heard his mom come in, and turn off all the lights with a half-hearted tut, then come in to kiss him goodnight while he pretended to be asleep. Even then, he slept badly, dreaming of strange shadowy figures with blank faces who appeared in his apartment before vanishing, inexplicably, over and over again.

JOSEPH WOOLF

1 July 1969

The next morning Jamie wrote his mom a note explaining that he was meeting some friends straight after his route, so he couldn't come back to see her. This was sort of true; it was better than the lying he would have to do if he saw her, anyway. And he knew that she would be pleased to hear he was making friends, so maybe she wouldn't be *too* disappointed. He tried not to think about it.

Then he annoyed Lou as usual, and did his route as usual, before very unusually finding a payphone to call

Long Island Jail.

He was told that visiting hours were between four p.m. and six p.m., but first he would need to fill out forms 1A, 1B, 3, 3.9 and XIVii. So he rang Rose and Eve, and arranged to meet them there at midday, with plenty of pens.

Then he was outside and back on the bike. He had one other visit to make before he went to the jail. The idea had come to him that morning: if he was going to work out why Vinnie's boss had burned down a dozen buildings, then he should find out who those buildings belonged to. And for that, he needed to pay a visit to the Office of the Recorder of Deeds.

This is a very boring title for quite an interesting place, but you might not have guessed just looking at it. It was housed on a boring, deserted road in a boring, deserted office that contained a boring, deserted man, and a lot of filing cabinets, and very little else. The files were all sorts of records of New York City: who had been born and who had died, who had married whom, and who had bought and sold land. Land, and buildings.

"Please," said Jamie, "I've come to ask about some

property deeds. I want to know who owns these buildings." And he handed a list of the buildings burned by the Arsonist to the man, who cast a weary eye down the paper. His eyes were very bulging, which magnified their weariness. He looked like a frog who has long ago had his fill of flies and lily pads and slime, and has given up hoping that there might ever be anything else to look at.

But at any rate, he took Jamie's list and made an affirmative sort of "Ahrrrm". Then he went ahrrrming off into a back room to find the right files to answer Jamie's query.

He took some time – long enough for Jamie to read every poster in the place twice, pace the room four times, sit down and stand up again five times, and slightly knock over a hatstand. At last, he came ahrrrming back again, Jamie's list in hand.

"Harry Hooper," he said, pointing to the first building on the list. He ran his fingers down the others one by one. "Harry Hooper, Harry Hooper, Harry Hooper, Harry Hooper. *Ahrrrm*. Harry Hooper . . . Harry Hooper, Harry Hooper, Harry Hooper . . . Harry

Hoo – *ahrrrm* – per."

Jamie gaped at him.

"*Ahrrrm*," he explained solemnly.

"Yes," said Jamie vaguely. "Thank you."

He had got it backwards. Harry Hooper was not the villain. *He was the victim.* The paper had said that Irena's show had been the most expensive show of the year; and who would be losing money refunding all the tickets? Harry Hooper. Who had lost ten buildings to the Arsonist's fires? Harry Hooper. Was somebody trying to bleed his fortune dry? A rich and powerful man like Harry must have plenty of enemies.

Could they even, he wondered, have been trying to shoot at Harry last night, not the mayor? He would have to see what Woolf could tell them.

At last, Jamie had a hunch about *why*. Now, *who*?

He had gone back outside and was in the middle of unchaining his bike when it hit him. There was an obvious Somebody who stood to gain if Harry Hooper lost too much money, and couldn't keep spending money on the *Yorker* to keep its prices low and sales high. Somebody who might even be willing to try and bump him off, if it meant that *she* could "run this city" in his place. And she was a blonde woman.

And, of course, she could own that lighter! How had he not seen it? There had been a statue of the candle and hourglass right there in her hallway! The crest of the *Yorker* was also *the crest of the Hooper family.*

Jamie's heart pounded. He was desperate to share his idea with someone. But he *really* couldn't tell Eve that he thought Vinnie's boss might be Pearl Hooper-Banks.

He was deep in thought as he kicked off on his bike, and still deep in thought when he arrived. The day was hot, but overcast; clouds crouched low and grey over the prison, which in turn crouched low and grey over Brooklyn. It was an enormous building, barely punctured by its tiny windows. It reminded Jamie of Vinnie's blank face.

He could see a small figure walking towards him, buckling under the weight of enough bags for a small army.

"Hi, Rose," said Jamie. "That's a lot of shopping."

Rose put down the bags she held in her left hand, then her right hand; then she eased some off her back, then off her front. "Brother, that's better. I had to do errands for a few neighbours and there wasn't time to take it all home first."

Jamie had once done an elderly neighbour's shopping, and he had felt very virtuous for about a month. By the looks of things, Rose had run errands for half of Harlem.

Next to arrive were Eve and Pumpkin. Late, of course. Then the three children picked up Pumpkin and all of Rose's bags, and approached the grey jail.

Inside the clerk's office – which was also grey – they were handed an enormous stack of paperwork, which they had to fill in if they wanted to see a prisoner. Filling out the forms took ages and ages and ages. Then they all had to read a list of things they mustn't take with them into prison, and sign it. Rose had to leave behind all the sorry-you're-in-prison presents she had brought for Joseph Woolf.

"No livestock," said Eve. "Do you think Pumpkin counts as livestock?"

They all looked at him. He did his best impression of a cushion. They agreed that he could probably get away with it, until Rose pointed out that the list also said "No cushions".

So they signed everything, and Eve went to tie Pumpkin up next to Jamie's bike. Then they all sat down and waited to be called.

The wait seemed interminable. Time in the prison was measured out and regulated, so that you could never forget it, even for a moment. A clock ticked loudly. Bells kept ringing, and whenever they rang, distant gates would clang and footsteps would sound, and sometimes lights on timers would turn themselves on or off; and then there would be silence again, apart from the whine of the fluorescent light in the waiting room.

While they waited, Jamie told them all that he had learned about the *why*. He left out his theory about the *who*, because he wasn't quite sure how to bring that up with Eve yet.

"So," he concluded, "Harry lost a fortune over the actress, and he lost a fortune over the buildings, and it *might* have been Harry that the bullet was meant for. This is all to do with getting at Harry. Trying to bankrupt him; maybe trying to kill him."

The others were gratifyingly excited. Rose's eyes grew and grew until they almost filled up her huge glasses, and Eve didn't get distracted once.

Then Eve showed them her work on the *how*. She had filled three notebooks, and there were also a lot of napkins and pillowcases and bits of wallpaper, from when an idea had suddenly struck her and she had just written it down on the nearest thing she could find.

"I've been trying to work out how the Arsonist disappeared from the buildings every time, and the actress disappeared from her dressing room," she said. "We know they're connected, so maybe the same trick was used. But," she sighed, "I haven't had much luck. I've been looking at all the burned buildings, and the Angel. I've looked at every possible way out, and I've run through all the timings. And I just don't see how any of them got away without being seen. It can't be done."

But evidently it *had* been done.

"And then," she continued thoughtfully, "there's vanishing act number three: the assassin. The gun was found on the sixth floor of the building. Woolf was on the sixth floor when the shots were fired, and didn't see anybody leaving. So whoever *really* shot the mayor vanished – *if* Woolf is telling the truth." She opened one of the notebooks. "I was wondering if maybe the gun could *actually* have been fired from a different floor, and the one in the room was a plant, but I can't see where else you could possibly get a clear shot from. Unless…" Her eyes went dreamy, and she was just explaining a particularly complicated theory showing that it *might* have been possible to shoot the bullet from a different floor and deflect it through the window with a trampoline, when they were finally called to the visitors' room. Jamie was privately relieved, as he hadn't really understood a word of that last bit, and his neck was aching a bit from nodding along wisely.

They followed a guard along years of grey corridor to the visitors' room, where prisoners waited behind panels of glass.

Jamie reminded himself that he was a reporter, and reporters had to be fearless. He reminded himself that Woolf might be innocent. He reminded himself that there was a good thick bit of glass between him and the prisoner. But something about the scowling face of Joseph Woolf still gave him the heebie-jeebies.

He was a small, wiry man, and surprisingly young. From his pale face, Jamie guessed he hadn't slept since his arrest. As he sat there, he was flipping a quarter, again and again and again.

He looked up as they approached, and smiled, but it wasn't a reassuring smile. It split his face open like a jack-o'-lantern.

"Three children!" he said. "What a surprise. I wondered what I was getting three of. Three wise men? Three bears? Three blind little mice? But it's three kiddywinks."

"Hello," said Jamie. "We've come—"

"Jamie Creeden," said Joseph, stabbing the glass with a well-bitten fingernail. "You're easy. But which is Rose, and which is Eve, hmm?" He flipped the quarter, made a face at the result and stabbed a finger at Eve. "A hoity-toity name like Hooper-Banks," he said, "belongs with a hoity-toity young lady like you. You're Eve." The finger moved. "You're Rose."

"Yes," said Jamie, "and we—"

"Well," said Joseph, his smile gone, replaced by the scowl again. "And what do three little piggies like you want with big bad Joseph Woolf, hmm? I thought I was meant to be New York's biggest villain now?"

"We've come because we don't think you tried to shoot the mayor," said Jamie quickly. "We think you were set up, and we think the person who did it is behind some other crimes in New York, and we want to know who they are and what they're up to."

"Is that right?" he said, looking at them properly for the first time. For a moment the scowl slipped, and there was something almost pleading in his expression. Then he looked away, and flipped the coin again. "Heads. Heads I win, tails I lose. I've been playing pretty much non-stop since I got put in this place, to stop myself going CRAZY!" This last word he shouted, then hit himself on the head, as if to demonstrate what a well-functioning head it was. "I'm trying," he continued, "to work out whether I'm a lucky man. So far, I've not been winning, not even once. Right now I'm losing one thousand, three hundred and twenty-three heads to one thousand, three hundred and twenty-four tails. So I guess I'm *not* a lucky man."

There was a silence at that. Then Joseph leaned forward. The smile was back. "But now," he said, "you three lucky billy goats gruff think you might just solve this riddle, hmm?"

"We're going to try," said Jamie firmly.

"Even though," Eve said earnestly, "you do look tremendously guilty, because I've been looking at the timings, and—"

"How about you tell us *your* version of events, Mr Woolf?" cut in Jamie.

"You can shut your eyes, if it would help," suggested Rose.

"Or not, if you don't want to," said Jamie, who was beginning to wish he had come alone.

Joseph shrugged, smile gone again. "I've already told the same spiel to the police, to the press, to my lawyers – everyone. You want it again, hmm? Well, why not. That's all I'm good for now." And he recited, flatly, "My shift was over. As I left I remembered we'd had this electrician in earlier that day, and I wanted to check they'd cleared up properly. So I turned back, and there I was in the library alone at 9.30, when I should have been at home. Which doesn't—" Here his voice wobbled unexpectedly, as though it was carrying something heavy and had lost its balance. He took a deep breath, scowled extra fiercely, and continued: "Which doesn't look so good for me, does it? Anyways. When I heard the gunshot, I was walking along the sixth floor corridor, and half a minute later I found the gun in that room, right by that open window. But I didn't see anybody coming *out* of the room, and if my story's true, then I should've seen them. So," he said, flipping the coin again angrily (heads), "you're absolutely right, Miss Hooper-Banks." He put on a cruel impression of her voice. "I look tre*meeend*ously guilty."

"Mr Woolf," said Jamie, "Harry Hooper was in the room too, wasn't he? How do we know the assassin was trying to shoot the mayor? Is there any solid proof?"

"The paper said that they missed by quite a few inches," supplied Eve. "Even if the bullet seemed closer to the mayor, surely it could have just been a bad shot?"

Joseph stopped worrying at the coin, and for a moment, he was still. "Well now," he said, "that's a smart question. The police asked just the same thing. The men had been sitting at the same table having drinks, pretty close to each other, so it didn't seem too clear cut."

Jamie felt a bubble of triumph. He *knew* it.

Woolf went on: "But then Mr Wilson said he'd gotten a threatening note just that morning, and it told him pretty straight that someone was going to get him that night. I saw it myself. Load of cut-up newspaper. Whoever put it together, they're as bad at spelling as shooting."

The children looked at each other. They knew those notes.

Eve sighed. "So I suppose we're back to square one."

"No, I don't think so," said Jamie thoughtfully. If that was the only evidence, then if anything, he was more certain now than before. "That story doesn't make any sense. Why warn somebody when you're going to go after them? That'd be stupid. *But* it would be a great decoy: if everyone thought that shooting Harry was an accident, the police would go looking in all the wrong places, for someone who hated the mayor."

Woolf leaned forward. There was something hungry in his expression. "Sure, that figures. It would be a smart move. But say, what've you got on this, hmm? What makes you think they were after Hooper?"

Jamie leaned forward too. He was excited now: man and boy had the same hungry expression, like a mirror image. "We think somebody has it in for him. Somebody who knows how to vanish, and keeps doing it. An arsonist has burned down ten of his buildings, and someone kidnapped an actress right before a show that he'd sold thousands of tickets for. We think they wanted to ruin him – maybe they tried to kill him too."

Joseph nodded slowly. "Interesting," he said. "Very interesting. But who...?"

"We're going to find out," said Rose earnestly. "And when we do, everything will be all right for you, you'll see."

Jamie did his best reliable face. "I'm going to write a piece about all of this for Young Reporter of the Year. We know about a guy called Vinnie who's involved, but we're looking for his boss, who we think might be a blonde woman." He wanted to mention Pearl, but for now he just said, "I've got some ideas."

Woolf nodded along. "Well," he said, "it's more than the police have bothered to find out, that's for sure. *Very* interesting." Then he flipped his quarter once again. Heads.

"Hey, would you look at that?" he said. His faced slashed open in his biggest smile yet.

"Heads!" said Rose. "Oh, good! That puts you out in front now, doesn't it?"

"Yes, it does, Miss Johnson," said Joseph. He leaned back in his chair and grinned hungrily at the three children. "Well, my three little musketeers," he said. "I don't know who you'll get to listen to your story – but it's something. It certainly is something. I wonder if you might just be about to bring me some luck after all."

INVASION!

1 July 1969

The three of them spent the evening in Prospect Park, lying on the grass, discussing everything that they had seen and learned. Jamie thought Woolf didn't seem entirely trustworthy, and Rose thought he seemed misunderstood and tragic, and Eve thought that all the timer-operated electronics in the prison had been very interesting. They talked until they were all talked out, and then they just lay there alongside the smell of the grass and the lengthening shadows, thinking.

It was Rose who broke the silence. "So what's the

plan, Jamie?"

Jamie carefully tied a knot in a blade of grass while he decided how to respond. He wanted to investigate Pearl, but he had to keep that to himself. "Let's meet tomorrow morning. We've got our *why*: I'll keep thinking about *who* would want to hurt Harry. Eve, you keep working on the *how* of the vanishing. Rose – do you think you could try again to find out from your dad what he saw? It would help so much."

Rose sighed. It was an enormous sigh, for such a small person. "I'll try. But I've asked so many times. He always just says, 'Nothing'."

Jamie turned his head to give her a comforting sort-of smile, and Pumpkin licked her face with extra slobber, which was probably meant to be nice. "Well," said Jamie, "thanks for trying, anyway."

Then Rose had to go and cook for her dad, and Eve had to go and report to her mother, so Jamie set off for home. He was too late for Pepe's, but he stopped at Memorial Pier for a while, leaning out over the railings. He felt something strange, but he couldn't quite name it.

As he looked at the distant lights of Manhattan, he thought about Eve and Rose, somewhere out there among the sprawling glitter. Eve would be going home to her mother right now; her mother, who might or might not be behind the city's biggest crime spree, obsessed with the downfall of her own brother. Rose would be going home to her broken father, to their run-down house where they didn't have enough money to get by. And then Jamie realized what that strange feeling was. He was worried about his friends. He had never had to worry about anyone besides his mom and himself before. It was an uncomfortable sort of worry, because there wasn't much he could *do* about it.

He set off home.

The silence was waiting again as soon as he opened his front door. There was a slight draught that might have been a breath; a faint creak that might have been a step. But Jamie was not going to scare so easily tonight. He stepped inside, shut the door, and turned on the light.

There was a blonde woman in the apartment.

She was casually sitting at his kitchen table, and

casually tapping her manicured fingers on the tabletop, and casually aiming a pistol at his chest. Her white-blonde hair was coiffed up in a swirl. She looked like an unusually dangerous Mr Whippy ice cream.

"Don't yell," said Cindy Bell calmly, "or I shoot."

Jamie didn't yell. But inside, he was screaming.

"Well," she went on, looking him up and down, "you're not what I was expecting at all. This *is* a surprise, sweetie."

"Ungg," said Jamie, who was fairly surprised himself.

What was most surprising to him, somehow, was how normal everything else was. The peeling yellow paint was still there, as normal; the table wobbled slightly, as normal; a very normal cockroach scuttled across the linoleum on its normal cockroachy business. Cindy Bell sat there with her pistol, but the apartment wasn't bothered; it just carried right on existing.

That made it worse, somehow. It was his *home*, in all its drab normalness. It wasn't meant to contain surprising news anchors with guns.

"Sit down," said Cindy – and Jamie's limbs obeyed, which was fortunate, since Jamie's brain was apparently busy. She considered him. "Just a kid, aren't you, sweetie?" She frowned. "So this can't be right. It must be your mommy or daddy I want. I don't suppose you'll tell me what time they'll be back." She waited, but Jamie didn't respond. "Well, I guess us two can just wait, and you can be good and not say a word." Her nails drummed a tattoo of impatience on the Formica; her heel kept time on the linoleum. (The cockroach paused its normal cockroachy business to look at that clicking heel in wonder. It was so lustrously shiny. It clicked so smartly.)

Jamie managed to get his voice working. "Excuse me," he said. "I'm sure it's not my mom you want. If you want anyone, it's probably me."

Cindy Bell raised her eyebrows. The cockroach sidled shyly over to her heel.

"You?" she said. "*You've* gotten mixed up in this?"

"Well, I think so," said Jamie, who wasn't one hundred per cent sure what *this* was yet. But his brain was slowly piecing it together. A blonde woman who hated Harry Hooper. Of *course*. Pearl was Harry's rival because she wanted the *Yorker*, but Cindy was his rival because she wanted to destroy it. The *Yorker* was the only serious competition left for *Goodnight, New York*, and it was winning. Jamie felt stupid for not thinking of Cindy earlier.

She leaned back and considered him. He waited. He had never watched someone so intensely before: the pistol certainly focused his mind. His nerves jangled at every quiver of her coiffed-up hair; every twitch of a muscle under her black jacket; every whisper of a movement from her gold-tipped fingers.

"You're telling me," said Cindy, "that it was *you* who sent that brainless lump of muscle to threaten me?"

"Er," said Jamie. He had only just worked out what was going on, and now he was confused again. "No. Do you mean Vinnie? I thought *you* sent him to threaten *me*."

Cindy leaned forward; she moved a foot and nearly crushed the cockroach, who beat a hasty retreat. "I don't know his name. I just know he came to my place to try and scare me into stopping my investigations. But I don't scare so easily. I tailed him, and last night I saw him letting himself in here. So I figured I'd pay a little visit, and see who he was working with. And the answer is . . . you?"

Jamie's head spun. He had a lot of questions, but Cindy had the pistol, so he answered hers first. "We don't work together," he said. "He was threatening me, too. I swear. I can show you the note he left."

For a few moments, Cindy thought about this. Then she nodded. "Show me." And so, slowly, Jamie got up and led her to his room; and slowly, she followed, never lowering the pistol. He unpinned the note from the wall. She raised her eyebrows at the boxes full of *Yorker*s, and all the articles pinned to his walls, and the stacks of notebooks next to Jamie's bed. Then she looked at Vinnie's note, for a long time.

When she looked up at Jamie again, her eyes were less horrifyingly cold. There was something in her gaze that might have been respect.

"OK," she said. "Go sit down again." Jamie did, and Cindy followed. Then she said, "Explain."

So Jamie did. And once he started talking, he felt an enormous wave of relief, and he didn't want to stop.

He talked about Bud's phone call and the vanished

Russian actress. He told her about Vinnie. He explained that Vinnie's boss was also behind the vanishing Arsonist, *and* the vanishing assassin; and that Harry Hooper was the target of all three crimes. He told her about the lighter, and the blonde woman Rose had seen. He told her about Pearl, who fitted with the lighter and the blonde woman; and who would have reason to bankrupt and maybe even kill Harry, to get the *Yorker* for herself.

Cindy was still listening intently, so he kept going. (The cockroach wasn't listening. It was busy trying to give Cindy's heel a gift of some interestingly clumped dust.)

He talked about Eve and Rose, his unexpected friends. He talked about his hopes of being a reporter, and the muddle of finding out that being a reporter was sometimes exhilarating but also sometimes terrifying, and how scared Vinnie's note had made him, but also how determined. He talked until his voice grew hoarse, and no more footsteps had passed outside for some time, and the lights of every other house in the street were turned off, and even the cockroach had decided that it might be time for bed.

And all the while Cindy Bell sat very still and listened, like an entirely unreadable Mr Whippy ice cream, pistol never wavering.

"So," Jamie concluded, "that's all of it, and it's the truth, I swear. Vinnie came around to threaten me because I was getting too close. You and me, we're on the same side."

Cindy gave him one last long, calculating look. Then she lowered the pistol.

"You," she said, "are quite some reporter, sweetie."

Jamie should have been mostly pleased about not dying, but to be honest, hearing those words in that famous honeyed voice was also pretty high up there on the pleased-ness scale.

"Pearl Hooper-Banks," murmured Cindy. "Makes a lot of sense – if she can get her paws on the *Yorker*, she'll call the shots in this city. I wouldn't be surprised if she's trying some underhand tactics to get it. I would!" She considered this, then said, "Well. It looks like I owe you an apology."

"It's OK," lied Jamie.

"No, sweetie, it's not. Having a pistol pointed at you's

no fun. I don't normally interview so rough, but the threats I've been getting have made me jumpy." And her fingers went back to the pistol – but only to put it away in the bag.

As she did so, Jamie saw her own Dictaphone in the bag, whirring away. He felt suddenly unsettled. But then, why shouldn't she? After all, she was a reporter, and she had come here for evidence.

Out of the bag, she took an envelope. She laid it on the table. "This Vinnie guy was trying to stop *my* investigations, too," she said. "I was just trying to do my job. Every time I try and get some kind of grip on these big stories, they just seem to slip out of my grasp. And the show's suffering. Between you and me, my job's on the line if I can't get something good soon. I've been given two more weeks to get our ratings back up, then I'm getting chucked out."

"So, I'm afraid your blonde woman probably *was* me – I followed Vinnie to the Johnsons' house. But this might interest you." And out of the envelope, she produced a photograph. "I had to snap this one fast, so it's not my best. But that's Vinnie, right? And could that be Pearl?"

The photograph was of a man and a woman, taken through a café window. The woman had her back to the window: if you didn't already know who you were looking for, it wasn't much to go on. But her golden curls were unmistakable.

"Wow," said Jamie. "Yes, that's Vinnie. With Pearl." He thought about this, and added, "Wow."

"Brilliant," said Cindy, sitting back with a smile. "Well, well. Pearl Hooper-Banks. That is quite *something.*" She tapped her nails on the photograph thoughtfully. "Listen, sweetie. I need to do some thinking about your theory – work out how it all fits together – see if I can find any proof. Once I do, I'll be in touch. I'll make sure you get the credit you deserve for this!" She put out a hand for Jamie to shake. "OK?"

"OK," said Jamie – which was an understatement – and shook it.

She put the photograph back in its envelope, and the envelope back in her bag, then checked her watch. "Your mommy and daddy ever coming home, sweetie?"

Jamie checked his own watch. He was amazed to see how long they had been talking; as it had happened, time had seemed frozen. "Any minute!"

"And I'm guessing," said Cindy, allowing herself a half-smile, "that they don't know about your little adventures?"

"No," said Jamie, uneasily. "It's not like I'm lying," he added hastily. "But she's not here much. She works really hard. And I don't want to worry her. So..."

"It's OK, sweetie, it's OK. No one ever approves of the things that people like us do until we make a success of them. It's probably for the best to keep it to yourself for now."

People like us. *People like us.* Jamie's face flushed with pride.

"Well then. I'd better get out of here, so I don't blow your cover." She stood. The heel clicked; half-asleep under a cupboard, the cockroach waved an answering pincer of farewell. "I'll call you, but if you find out anything else, or you need any help, you call me, OK?" And Cindy Bell put a business card on the table. "Hey, you never told me your name."

"Jamie Creeden," said Jamie.

"Jamie Creeden," said famous-news-anchor-Cindy-Bell. "I have a feeling I'll be seeing that name on the front page before too long." And she clicked her way to Jamie's front door and gave him her first full smile of the night. It was a fierce sort of smile. Then she was gone, her spiral of hair whirling out into the night, the door smartly clicking shut behind her.

For a minute Jamie just watched the door, frozen.

People like us.

That was what Cindy had said. That had been wonderful.

Plus, he was very much still alive. He felt a rush of euphoria.

But as he sat and waited for his racing heart to slow, other thoughts crowded in. So now he *knew* that Pearl was in cahoots with Vinnie. Which meant she was almost certainly responsible for kidnap and arson and attempted murder.

How on earth was he going to tell Eve?

His mind couldn't cope with so much to think about at once. In a daze, he went to bed, but he didn't sleep. He sat with the covers drawn up to his chin, thinking thoughts so overwhelmingly big that they didn't quite fit inside words and had to be thought without them. He heard his mom come in, and it took all his strength not to call out to her.

He heard the thick silence that comes deep in the middle of the night. Then he heard the birds singing, telling him that the world was starting again. He thought of the *Yorker* candle, burning down and starting again, over and over and over.

Today, he would have to speak to Eve.

PAPERBOY IN DISGRACE

2 July 1969

Jamie could not wake in the dark as usual, because he was already awake, but he got up at the usual time to begin again. Before he could bother Lou as usual and do his route as usual, he found the note that had been shoved under his front door. Vinnie, paying him another call.

BACK off JAMIE, Or theRe wIll be TRUbLe. FOR Eve to tHIs TiME.

He stood very still, looking at that note. If he was right, and Vinnie *was* working for Pearl, then Eve was in real danger. Surely Pearl wouldn't order him to harm her own daughter? She was bluffing. Or was she?

He picked up the papers and raced impatiently through his route. That day the flowers in Mrs Darling's garden were drooping a little in the heat, and the ride to Eve's apartment felt long and sweltering. It seemed to Jamie that the flags of traffic lights on Fifth Avenue spent an unreasonable amount of time being red.

When Jamie at last arrived at Eve's building and went up to her apartment, he could hear clarinet scales through her front door, floating up and down. Up and down, up and down, up and down. He paused before knocking, and listened. The playing sounded so tranquil. He almost didn't like to disturb it.

But he knocked anyway.

Eve answered with her very dreamiest look on, then saw it was Jamie and smiled. "Oh, hello! Any news?"

He hesitated. "Is your mother in?"

"No, but she'll be back any minute."

"We need to talk first." Jamie stepped inside.

Pumpkin shuffled up to say hello and eat his shoelaces affectionately.

"Are you all right?" said Eve. "You look awful. What is it?"

"Well," said Jamie. "The thing is. You see." He got a grip on himself. "Do you know who Cindy Bell is?"

"The news anchor, yes."

"Right," said Jamie. "Look. I've got something to tell you." And he told the whole tale of the night before, and everything he had worked out about Pearl, without pulling any punches. The more he told, the more intensely Eve seemed to be paying attention. He didn't think he had ever seen her like that before. Her grey eyes looked at him with the full force of her intelligence. It was a bit much. When he had finished speaking, there was a short silence.

"Just to be very clear," said Eve slowly. "A woman broke into your apartment and held you at gunpoint last night. She is a blonde woman who has every reason to try and ruin Uncle Harry, so she's exactly what we're looking for. But you do not suspect her. Actually, you think she is super. You think she is so super that you have *told her all about us.*"

Jamie paused. He hadn't looked at it that way. "Well. I don't think—"

"And," continued Eve, "while Cindy is now your new best friend, you think *my mother* is a lying thieving kidnapping fire-setting criminal who tried to murder her own *brother?*" By the end of the sentence, Eve's voice was loud. Very loud. The sort of loud that made Pumpkin hunker down under all his fur and think about hiding there for approximately the next couple of years.

"Er," said Jamie, "well, you *did* always say she was a bit controlling..."

"Oh my God, Jamie."

"Are you OK?"

"No, you idiot, I am furious. Obviously I am furious."

Jamie had been worried about upsetting her. He had been worried about frightening her. He hadn't really considered that he might make her *angry*. "Eve," he protested, "I'm telling you as a friend."

"Jamie, I don't think you know a lot about friendship—"

"Oh, and you do?" It was a low blow; Jamie could feel he was losing control.

"Oh, whatever. I know *neither of us* know a lot about friendship – happy? – but I'm going to go out on a limb and say that friends don't normally accuse each other of having corrupt murderous families just to get their own ace reporter kicks."

This was so unfair that Jamie could only splutter – which was infuriating, because there were about a hundred biting and articulate things he wanted to say, if he could only get his mouth to work.

Just then, Rose arrived.

"Hello hello!" she said, knocking on the open door.

Jamie looked at her. Eve looked at her. She looked from one to the other.

"Um," she said, "I brought cookies?"

There was no time for anyone to decide what to say about cookies, because the next person to waltz through the door was Pearl Hooper-Banks. Her icy smile froze when she saw Jamie, and practically dripped icicles when she saw Rose.

"Jamie. What a surprise, dear," she said. "And

151

this is…?"

Pearl *mustn't* find out that Rose was Art Johnson's daughter. Jamie tried to give Rose a look that said *don't say your surname whatever you do*, but that is quite a lot to say just with a look. He only really managed to look like a strangled fish, which unsurprisingly didn't stop Rose from saying, "Rose Johnson."

"Charming," said Pearl, her voice plummeting to well below zero. "Change into something smarter, Eve dear, and ask your friends to leave. Grandfather has announced that he's coming for lunch right away – and invited your uncle Harry and his friends, although Lord knows how he expects me to produce lunch with no notice, I had to persuade Macy's to send a delivery…"

"Jamie! Well, what a surprise, kid!" Harry Hooper appeared in the doorway next. "And who's this?" he said to Rose.

Jamie did his strangled fish face again, but, "Rose Johnson," said Rose.

Harry was shortly followed by a tiny old man with astonishing eyebrows. "God, this place is much too shiny," he announced. "Pearl! I'm here! What's for lunch? Can you get jelly? I'm in the mood for strawberry jelly."

"Hello, Grandfather," said Eve.

"You've gotten taller again," muttered Grandfather Hooper, eyebrows plummeting in annoyance. "Stop that. Do *you* know if your mother's got any strawberry jelly? Who are these two? Do *they* have jelly?" He fixed Jamie with a ferocious stare. "Well? Do you?"

"No, sir," said Jamie. "I'm Jamie Creeden. This is Rose."

"Jamie Creeden!" The eyebrows soared again. "I've heard that name. Isn't that the paperboy you were telling me about, Harry? The one you thought had something? Well, then you must stay! You must both stay! Pearl. *Pearl*. Listen, girl. We're going to need more jelly. These two are staying."

"Really, Father—" began Pearl – but then Grandfather Hooper began humming the James Bond theme to himself and looking out of the window, eyebrows dancing in time to the humming, and that seemed to be the end of *that*. Jamie glanced at Eve, but she glared at him so fiercely that he quickly looked away again. There was a frosty silence.

"I brought cookies," offered Rose.

"Aha!" said Grandfather Hooper. "Finally, someone who talks sense around here."

And so it was that Jamie found himself at lunch with Eve, Rose, Pearl, Harry, Grandfather Hooper and their friends – who just happened to be the chief of police and the mayor of New York, which was apparently no big deal. The mayor looked like a bull who had accidentally got trapped in a suit. The chief of police looked like a very small man who had accidentally got trapped on a very large moustache.

As if it wasn't already surreal enough, the dining room had large mirrors on all four walls, which were reflecting each other, and showed hundreds of Jamies and Eves and Roses and Pearls and Harrys and Grandfathers and mayors and chiefs, on and on endlessly. Countless Eves glared at countless Jamies. He was trapped in an infinite anger loop.

He was not the only one. The atmosphere at the table was thick with anger. Pearl and Eve bickered.

Pearl and Harry bickered. The mayor and the chief of police seemed to hate each other; whenever one said "Yes, yes", the other would quickly say "No, no", and vice versa. As for Rose, the pain of so many unhappy people at once thoroughly muddled her, and she spent the whole meal looking from face to bitter face in anguish.

The atmosphere was not improved by the discovery that the Macy's delivery did not, in fact, include any strawberry jelly. After that the only one having a good time was Pumpkin, who had a whole forest of ankles to nibble hopefully at.

"Anybody for a cheese tartlet?" said Pearl.

"Yes, yes," said the chief of police.

"No, no," roared the mayor.

"I hate cheese tartlets," said Grandfather Hooper.

"Really, Pearl," said Harry, "you *know* he hates cheese tartlets."

"*Thank* you, Harry," fumed Pearl.

"I *love* cheese tartlets," said Rose, taking two to make Pearl feel better. "And this juice is really nice, isn't it?"

"Yes, yes," roared the mayor.

"No, no," murmured the chief of police, moustache billowing in disagreement.

Wurf, said Pumpkin.

The telephone rang. Pearl got up to take the call. It felt like the end of a round, but it was very unclear who had won a point.

While she was gone, Jamie seized his chance. He was still upset about the argument with Eve, but he couldn't let that throw him when there was a job to do. He had the opportunity to interview the mayor and Harry Hooper in one fell swoop. He thought of poor Irena Dragunova and Art Johnson and Joseph Woolf and Cindy Bell, and tried not to look at Eve. In his pocket, he turned on the Dictaphone.

"Mr Mayor, sir," he said, "I read about what that Woolf guy did. Boy, that must have been scary, getting shot at like that."

"Yes, yes," agreed the mayor.

"No, no," said the chief of police, who hadn't really heard what they were talking about, because some of his moustache had got caught in his ear.

"And for you, Mr Hooper," said Jamie. "You were there too, weren't you?"

Harry looked a bit startled at the turn the conversation had taken. Eve gave Jamie a poisonous look over the potato salad.

"Boy, that would have been terrible. I mean, if something had happened to you, then what would happen to the *Yorker*?"

Grandfather Hooper broke in. "The *Yorker* doesn't need Harry. It's bigger than any of us. Pearl would take care of it."

Pearl walked into the room at this point, and gave Grandfather a winning, almost-warm smile. "I might even sell some copies," she said sweetly.

"Pearl," said Harry, his cheeks flushing angrily, "as you *well* know, sales have increased *significantly* over the last year, and—"

"BORING," yelled Grandfather. "Save it for the board meeting."

"ISN'T THE WEATHER WONDERFUL?" cried Rose, who was fast approaching a meltdown from all the bitterness.

There was a minute's tense silence, during which nobody answered Rose's question, and everybody chewed tartlets and salad and cocktail sausages aggressively at each other.

"*I'd* like to talk about Cindy Bell, Uncle Harry," said Eve suddenly. "Her show is doing very badly, isn't it? She must hate you and the *Yorker*."

"Oh yes – old foes," chuckled Harry. "She loathes me, I'm afraid."

And Eve made *You see?!* eyebrows at Jamie.

"Well, I'd like to talk about the Arsonist!" Jamie half-shouted. "It was all your buildings they burned, wasn't it, Mr Hooper? That seems like *inside knowledge* to me."

"Uncle," Eve semi-yelled, "do you remember that lovely Christmas we had last year, and the beautiful crystal typewriter mother gave you? I love how even though we all squabble, we're still *family*."

"Mr Hooper," cried Jamie, "who would you say is your main rival? The person who wants to run the *Yorker* instead of you?"

"Well, goodness," laughed Harry, "I feel like I'm

being interviewed."

"That's because you *are*," yelled Eve. "He thinks he's going to be a reporter, even though he's just an uneducated nobody…"

To Jamie's own surprise as much as anyone's, he appeared to be standing up, as he shouted, "Well, *you're* just a stuck-up, spoiled little girl who can't see…"

But he never finished the sentence. As he stood, the Dictaphone fell out of his pocket, and landed on the ground with an awkward clatter. Everybody peered down to see what it was. It lay there innocently, tiny tape wheels spinning behind their little plastic cover. There was a horrible, stony silence.

It was Pearl who broke the silence at last, in a soft voice, which Jamie could tell at once was her most dangerous. "Jamie," she said, "have you been recording us? In my family home? Where you are a guest?"

And Jamie just nodded, because the Dictaphone was lying there for everybody to see, and there wasn't anything else he could say.

The mayor forgot to glare at the chief of police and Harry forgot to glare at Pearl and Grandfather Hooper forgot to glare at the cheese tartlets. For one brief, awful moment, they were all united in glaring at Jamie.

Rose widened her eyes at him in maximum sympathy. But Eve would not look up from her plate.

"I think," said Pearl, *very* softly, "that it would be best if you left now."

"I—"

"Jamie," said Harry, "please don't argue with my sister." He was looking at Jamie with grave disappointment.

Jamie looked at Eve, but she was looking at her plate. He felt thoroughly humiliated, and thoroughly abandoned, and it seemed as if his heart was throbbing somewhere just behind his temples instead of in his chest where it belonged. There were hot tears in his eyes.

"Thank you for lunch," he said, with as much dignity as he could manage.

Nobody replied. Jamie picked up his Dictaphone and left the apartment. In the mirrors, a hundred Eves watched him go, without saying a word.

RETURN OF THE PAPERBOY

2 July 1969

Jamie stood outside the apartment building. He was not used to either anger or embarrassment. Both at once was . . . muddling.

The muddlingness was made worse by a faint twinge of doubt. *Had* he been too hasty, trusting Cindy? No; he was sure it was Pearl that was behind all this. Every line of enquiry led back to her. But if he was going to win Eve back over, he would need some kind of proof. He knew *who* – Pearl Hooper. He knew *why* – to destroy her brother and his empire, and take over the *Yorker*. But he didn't know *how*. That was meant to be Eve's job; but it looked like he was on his own now. A nearby pigeon pecked inquisitively at his foot. "HEY," bellowed Jamie. The pigeon flapped off immediately, and a nervous young man strolling past gave a whimper and broke out into a trot. As he watched the man go trotting and trembling off, and the pigeon lumber sadly away from him, it occurred to Jamie that maybe he needed to pull himself together.

He had never imagined that being a reporter would be this lonely. First he had cut off his mom, now his friends. He wondered if Bud had ever been lonely. And where he was now: hiding somewhere? Frightened away, for knowing too much?

For the first time, it struck Jamie that Bud Finkleby must have known more than anybody else in New York about the vanishing villains. They were his stories, after all. And even if he had gone, he must have had tapes or notes or *something*.

Without really noticing himself make the decision, he found he was back on his bike, and pointing it towards the *Yorker* headquarters. He told himself that he was going to check Bud's files, in case his research had not yet been thrown away. And this *was* a good idea. But if he was one -hundred-per-cent-completely-honest, he was also just desperate to sit in the candlelight and the coffee-scented air, surrounded by the hustle of the paper, and feel a bit less alone.

He hardly thought about the road as he cycled back downtown. Around him, a lot of angry horns suggested that maybe he *should* think about it, at least a bit, but he didn't hear them.

The *Yorker* statue was waiting when he arrived, proud and impassive. He wasn't going to try and reason with the receptionist again, so he waited until a group of researchers *fwmph*ed in together, then joined the back of the crowd and crossed the foyer without her noticing. The others waited for the elevator, but he went straight for the stairs, two at a time, up to Six P.M.

At the reporters' floor, the flame was still a few floors above him, and it was bright and cheerful. Rod and Ted and Todd and Ed and Judd and Ned and Chad all recognized him, and said friendly hellos. It didn't seem to occur to any of them that he might have come here uninvited. It felt good to be back where he belonged, with fellow reporters in the warm light.

Bud Finkleby's desk had not been cleared. His pots of hair oil and shoe polish were still there, and his typewriters and notebooks. It was a very tidy desk.

Jamie flicked through the notebooks. They were almost empty. Did Bud ever do *any* work?

He tried the desk drawers. The top drawer was full of all Bud's articles, lovingly clipped out from the final newspaper and stored away, on top of a pile of fan mail and some signed photos of his own face. Jamie rifled through the articles – telephone interviews with Irena from the run-up to her show; eyewitness interviews of the fires; all things Jamie had pored over before. They weren't useful.

The second drawer had a few scraps of paper – mostly shopping lists – and the note from the Voice that Jamie had seen before. He reread it:

MR FINKLEBY,

I HAVE INFORMATION ABOUT IRENA DRAGUNOVA. I SAW WHAT REALLY HAPPENED THAT DAY. THERE WAS NO MAGIC TRICK: THIS IS THE REAL WORLD, AND REAL PEOPLE DON'T JUST VANISH INTO THIN AIR!

I WILL CALL YOU TONIGHT, BUT I WILL ONLY BE ABLE TO CALL ONCE, AND I DON'T KNOW WHEN. PLEASE BE BY YOUR TELEPHONE TO TAKE THE CALL. YOU DON'T WANT TO MISS THIS!

YOURS IN GOOD FAITH.

He read it again, but it didn't get any more useful.

The final drawer had an address book, and nothing else. Jamie checked the hair oil, just in case it was some sort of fabulous cover for a stash of top-secret evidence. It wasn't. It was hair oil. Bud Finkleby was officially the world's most useless reporter.

He was just feeling despondent when he realized, in a burst of inspiration, that if Bud had interviewed Irena over the telephone, her number must be in his address book. Who would answer now, if you called it? Her family? Her agent? A lead, certainly! He grabbed the book out of the drawer.

He looked under D.

He looked under I.

He thumbed the whole thing through, from front to back. It made no sense. Why hadn't Bud got a number for her?

In fact, wasn't it a bit strange that there were absolutely *no* notes at all about her on his desk? How had he written any of the stories? Jamie looked around at the teetering piles of paper on the other reporters' desks. Bud had reported on Irena for weeks in the run-up to her show. Why was there *nothing*?

He unfolded the headline about her disappearance, one last time, and laid it next to the Voice's note. He felt a wave of despair. It was as though he was chasing ghosts, or thin air. He didn't even know what Irena Dragunova looked like – the photograph they had chosen for the front page that day was one of her arriving at the theatre, surrounded by five bodyguards, and he could only glimpse a hat and a slice of a dark coat.

Hold on. *Five* bodyguards? He scanned the article frantically. It mentioned six.

He had never stopped to look at the photo before.

Five bodyguards somehow became six bodyguards. And one actress somehow became zero actresses. Jamie wasn't great at maths, but even he could see where that was going.

He looked at the Voice's note again, and for the first time it struck him that the wording was strange. *Real people don't just vanish.* Real *people.*

What if Irena Dragunova wasn't real?

The only person who had spoken to Irena Dragunova was Bud Finkleby. New York only knew that she was famous in Russia because Bud Finkleby said so: it said right there in the article that only a select few Russians came to the USA, so people would have to take Bud's word for it. And Bud hadn't left behind a shred of evidence that he had ever talked to her. Could Jamie really be sure that there was any such person?

But there *had* been fires, and there *had* been gunshots. The Arsonist and the assassin had to be real – surely? Of course, no one ever actually *saw* the Arsonist...

...Well, except one person. He took Rose's number out of his pocket, then jammed his left hand over his left ear and the phone receiver over his right. There were four bleats of the phone before a man's voice answered. "Yes?" His voice was low and cautious.

"Mr Johnson? Art?"

"Yes?"

"Please, sir, this is a strange question, but – I promise I'm trying to help. The night you went to find the Arsonist in the fire. Was he ... real? Was there anybody there?"

There was a second's silence (except for Ed starting an argument with Judd at the desk behind, which was distracting), and then Art Johnson croaked, "N – oooh, I can't tell you that. I can't. Please – please, just leave me alone."

And with a muffled sob, he hung up.

Jamie felt a moment of triumph, because he was obviously right. But the triumph was quickly followed by confusion, because he didn't understand this at all. And confusion was followed in turn by guilt. The one thing Rose had asked of him was to stay away from her father.

Without pausing to think, he dialled Eve's number, to make things right with Rose. Pearl picked up.

"Oh, hello," said Jamie gruffly, improvising. "This

is Mr Kaminsky. I've remembered something very important about clarinet scales that I must tell Eve at once."

And Pearl sounded a *bit* puzzled by this, but it worked. Eve came to the phone.

"Eve, it's me. Don't hang up. Look, I just spoke to Art Johnson and—"

"Geez Louise, Jamie. She *asked* us not to. You and this stupid scoop. You're obsessed."

"I know. But I had to. Please just tell her for me, and tell her I'm sorry?"

"Mmm," said Eve, at her most vague.

Even though he was still kind of mad with her and she was kind of making him madder, Jamie wanted to talk to Eve about what he had learned. She was the only person he really trusted with it. "Don't you want to know what my idea was?"

"Not really."

"*None of them exist.* The Arsonist, the actress, the assassin. You were right, they couldn't have vanished. So they didn't. They were never there."

There was a pause: then despite herself, Eve

asked, "Then how were the fires started? And how was there a gunshot? And why did somebody make them up?"

"Still working on that," admitted Jamie, but at the same moment Judd started yelling at Ed, at top volume, so he had to say it again. "I said, STILL WORKING ON THAT."

"Sounds nuts, Jamie," said Eve. And she hung up.

Jamie listened to the hum of the phone, then slammed it down. But there was no time to be cross. He had to follow this last piece of the puzzle to its conclusion: when he could prove the truth to her, he could win her back round. And Rose too.

Judd and Ed were not helping. Judd was waving a lot of papers in Ed's face and ranting about some problem with a story, and Ed was trying to ignore him by building a small wall between them out of used coffee cups.

"*Look,*" yelled Ed in despair, when his cup wall finally collapsed. "If you want to try and rewrite the story now, then good luck to you. But I say we run it as it is. We don't have time to start over."

Jamie swivelled away from them, in the vain hope it

would block them out. Facing this way, he could see the great trunk of the candle through the window.

What did it mean? Why *invent* these people – and *how*? Was Pearl still behind it? Jamie dropped his head into his hands and groaned. (Ed was now yelling, "NO TIME, TICK, TOCK, NO TIME, TICK, TOCK," loudly at Judd, while Judd tried to reason with him.)

Jamie stared at the candle. A great globule of wax was running down its side. "TICK," yelled Ed, "TOCK."

"Shut *up*," yelled Judd.

"Oh!" yelled Jamie.

He stood up so fast, and with such an impressively loud clatter of his chair, that Ed and Judd stopped in mid-yell to look at him.

But Jamie wasn't paying any attention to them any more. Ed had nudged something in his brain; something that the candle clock was already loudly proclaiming. Eve had been right, back when she had first examined the stories. It *was* all in the timing.

Jamie scribbled down some figures on a piece of paper and stared at them, frowning. He wasn't great at maths. But he knew someone in this building who could tell him for sure whether he was right. So he ran out of the room, and went spinning downstairs around the candle clock, round and round that great monument to time, down to see Hal in the press room at Midnight.

THE CANDLE CLOCK

2 July 1969

Hal was not at Midnight when Jamie arrived. Nobody was. The lines and lines of linotype machines waited patiently. Next door, the printing press stood silent.

Jamie decided to wait five minutes. When the five was up he didn't have a better plan, so he waited for another five, and then a bit more. When fifteen minutes had passed, Hal came wandering in, slurping at some coffee and humming to himself. (It is tricky to do both at once. Hal was a particularly experienced slurp-hummer. Don't try this at home.)

"Jimmy!" he slurped-and-said, when he spotted Jamie. "You've come to visit again?"

"Uh-huh," said Jamie. It was not, technically, untrue. "Beautiful machines down here, Hal."

"Yessir," said Hal, stroking the nearest linotype absently. "They're doozies."

"Did you say that press could do two hundred thousand an hour?"

"Yup, when she's going full speed!"

"And there are five hundred thousand copies every night, right? By midnight on the dot?"

"On the *dot*. I'm never late."

"Not even a *bit* late?"

"Not a bit," said Hal, slurping proudly. "Like I told you, there's a whole carefully timed chain of workers and vans and delivery kids waiting – if we're delayed here, the whole operation goes wrong."

"So," said Jamie. He looked down at his sums. He had spent most of the fifteen minutes working and reworking them, and wishing Eve was there. He *thought* he was right, but he needed to check. "Five hundred thousand papers takes two and a half hours. So you go to print no later than nine thirty every night, right?"

Hal put down his coffee. He looked at Jamie, who tried and failed to look like someone with a casual interest in print times. Jamie wished that Hal would slurp or hum or both, but he just looked. Then he ran his hands through his sparse hair and exhaled loudly.

"Johnny," he said, "you're a good kid. I'm going to go right ahead and forget you asked that question. OK?" And he waited, arms folded, for Jamie to say "OK" back.

But it wasn't OK. Jamie began to pace and sketch in the air with his hands, unaware how much he looked like the reporters that he had so recently admired. "But Hal, there have been stories in the *Yorker* about things that happened after nine thirty, right? The actress that vanished, and the Arsonist, and the assassin who shot at the mayor . . . all those stories finish after nine-thirty, too late for them to have been written before the print deadline." He paused the pacing, frowning. "But the *Yorker* has never been late. So they *were* written before the print deadline. Which means *they were written before they happened.*"

"Really, Jamie—" pleaded Hal, glancing nervously

towards the door.

"So somebody at the *Yorker* already knew they were going to happen. Bud? They're all his stories…" Although, as he said it, he realized how strange it was that Bud had written the assassin story the night before he resigned – the night when he was meant to be having a drink with an old friend.

He had stared at those articles so many times. The times had been there all along. And Bud Finkleby's name had been right there, when Jamie knew perfectly well he was meant to be elsewhere that night. "So, wait. Did Bud . . . or…?"

"Best not to ask too many questions, Jamie," said Hal. "Really. Best just to keep quiet."

"But—"

"Really, Jamie, Hal's right," said Harry Hooper. "Quiet *would* be best. But you never were a very quiet boy, were you?"

Jamie turned to the doorway, where Harry stood. He wore the same gently wounded look that he had worn when the paper was late.

"Boss," said Hal, "please, go easy, he's just—"

"Hal," said Harry, "shut up. Jamie, would you follow me upstairs a moment, kid?"

Jamie weighed up what he knew so far. "Er," he said, "actually, I have to, um…"

Harry waved his hand, as if to say he quite understood about the need to *um*. "Ah well, swell, swell. You could just leave with my friend Vinnie now."

And at this signal, Vinnie appeared behind him, more enormous than Jamie had remembered. He glared at Jamie with those tiny eyes, and punched his palm menacingly.

"Ow," he said, slightly taken aback by his own strength.

"But," said Harry, "I was hoping we could have a little talk before things had to come to that." He walked in and placed a heavy hand on Jamie's shoulder. "I don't *want* to hurt you, Jamie. I want to explain. But if you insist on trying to leave here with half-baked notions in your head, then I will have to intervene."

Jamie looked at Hal. Hal was now taking an enormous and miserable interest in the nearest linotype.

He didn't trust Harry one bit. But he couldn't get past Vinnie. He had no choice but to play along for now, and try and find a moment to escape later. "OK," he said.

"Swell," said Harry. His smile was disarmingly warm. "That's just swell."

So Jamie, Harry and Vinnie went up in the elevator. Jamie didn't normally mind elevators, but right now his stomach was doing peculiar things, and the swoop upwards didn't help. He concentrated on the scorch marks of Eve's fire to steady himself. They stopped at Midday, and while Vinnie waited outside, Jamie and Harry went into Harry Hooper's office. Harry locked the door.

It was a magnificent office. One side looked over the candle, burning very far below now; opposite, a line of windows were open to let in the summer air, and all their windowsills were lined with glittering awards and framed photographs. Along a third side, huge windows let in a flood of light, showing a sweeping view of Manhattan. It felt like all Jamie's dreams come true, and not at all like a place where he should be horribly afraid. Harry sat down at a magnificent mahogany desk, flanked by a great brass hourglass on the left and a great brass lantern on the right.

"Sit down, Jamie," he said, "and let's talk this over." And he gestured for Jamie to sit opposite him. Jamie obeyed. His back was to the open windows, his face to the candle.

"So," said Harry. "You spotted our little game."

Jamie wasn't sure if he *had*, yet. It didn't make sense. "None of them are real people – no actress, no arsonist, no assassin. And the *Yorker* knew about all the crimes before they happened. So ... did you just ... make all those people up?"

Harry nodded. "And plenty of others. Cheeky, I know," he said, with a half-smile.

Jamie thought of Art Johnson cowering at home, and Joseph Woolf facing a life in jail, and Cindy Bell being threatened by Vinnie, and he *hated* Harry Hooper and his half-smile and his "cheeky". And he still didn't understand *how*.

But Harry kept right on talking, as though they were discussing a decision to change the font or lower the price. "We were in dire straits, Jamie. Papers up and down the country have closed. It was already bad, but once that charming Miss Bell started telling everyone the news at nine o'clock the night before, *nobody* wanted to buy it again the next morning. We were on the brink of collapse.

"An overnight bombshell, now *that* sells. We do some small ones, and some big – it sounds like you've cottoned on to some of our most sensational ones in your little investigation." He leaned back, and put his fingers into a pleased sort of steeple. "You're good."

Jamie disagreed. He wasn't good. He had been so close, but he had it all backwards. The Hooper rivalry for the paper *was* at stake, but he had been wrong to accuse Pearl. And he had *known* that they both wanted the paper for its power over people's thoughts; but never once had he thought that power might be being used on *him*.

He should have trusted in the obvious. If Bud didn't seem to be doing any real reporting work, then he wasn't. If people vanishing seemed to be impossible, then it was. What the three sensational bestselling headlines had in common was that they were three sensational bestselling headlines. And if there is a gigantic fiery candle clock running the length of a building, then you should probably pay attention to *time.*

No wonder Cindy had found the stories so impossible to report on: they were thin air.

"People want villains, Jamie," Harry went on. "They want outrage, scandal, gossip. So for a year now, we've delivered. Every other paper is failing, and we're booming – well, now you understand why."

But there was still so much Jamie *didn't* understand. "How?" he said. "I mean – the buildings *did* burn, people saw it…"

Harry liked that question. He leaned forward on his desk conspiratorially. "Oh yes, you have to give the people a show," he said. "But you can't *really* have someone in the burning buildings, or shooting at the mayor, or kidnapping an actress – they'd never get away. As you no doubt concluded, it's impossible. My rule is: spectacular crimes, imaginary criminals."

In Jamie's mind, the Voice scolded him: *Real people don't just vanish.*

"The trick, Jamie, is to set it all up early. Take the Arsonist. Eve put her finger on it the first time you met her, when the elevator caught fire – an electric current through a bare copper wire, as she so cleverly told us, is a fire hazard. Vinnie goes into the buildings as an electrician, and he attaches bare wire and a tape player to a timer switch. Much later, that switch turns on the tape player, and sends a current through the wire. The fire starts, the voice speaks, the violin plays – and by the time the fire has finished, all that evidence has been burned to cinders. Neat, isn't it?" He smiled. "That one's my favourite. As you probably know, it's gotten me more sensational headlines than any other trick I've played. Not to mention a healthy insurance payout on all the buildings, which was very welcome; between you and me, I've almost gone bust keeping this paper alive."

Jamie remembered the overalls Vinnie had been wearing, and the copper wire he had tied Jamie up with. It felt like years ago. He wished he had paid more attention when Eve had been admiring all the timer switches used in Long Island jail.

"So," said Jamie, "the electrician at Woolf's building was Vinnie too…"

"Yes, just an excuse to get him inside. He planted the gun over the road, then when it was time I fired my *own* gun, in our room, harmlessly into the wall. Mayor Wilson was more than happy to play our victim – it made him very popular, just around election time too… And," he added happily, "that particular story sold the highest number of papers on record."

Jamie nodded slowly. He thought of Eve, trying to work out where else the bullet could have been fired from to end up in that room. The only possibility that she hadn't considered was the room itself. Harry was warming to his theme now: there was something less dignified, almost childlike, about his glee. "As for the missing actress, she was easy. I made her up, I made her famous, I made her vanish." He smiled fondly at the memory. "So few Russians are allowed to travel here; if I tell people she's a Russian star, and give her weeks of hype in the paper, then who's going to contradict me? I tell the people what to think!"

Jamie was looking at Harry with a mixture of

amazement and disgust, which he seemed to misread as awe. He inclined his head graciously. "It's all my work, Jamie. That idiot Finkleby was happy enough to put his name to whatever I wanted to print; I told him I just wanted to keep my hand in with the reporting, anonymously. He didn't know it was all just invention. But the longer it went on, the more clues he stumbled across, and I was sure he *must* be getting suspicious. . . I was convinced he couldn't be as stupid as he seemed. The truth is, kid, I was getting paranoid. When I heard he was talking to a source at the Angel about Irena, I thought it might be time to . . . intervene."

Here, Harry adopted a look of great fatherly concern. "But of course, he sent *you* instead. I was furious, Jamie. Endangering you like that!" And he shook his head, as though Jamie getting abducted was really Bud Finkleby's fault, and not Harry Hooper's fault at all. "So I suggested to him that night that perhaps it was time for him to get the next train out of town and not come back. He was easily persuaded, once Vinnie had a word."

The smoke from the candle curled past the windows

as Harry spoke. Jamie had always believed, without hesitation, in the truth that candle stood for. He thought of his room piled high with *Yorkers*, and all the hours he had spent reading them, and all the reporters he had admired so much. He didn't want to stop believing in it all: what else was there to believe in?

"Do they all know?" he said. "Ed and Todd and Ted and . . . you know. . . Are they all in on it?"

"Oh, no," said Harry, dismissing the reporters with a wave of his hand. "The only ones who know exactly what time the press must be switched on are the press workers, and me. This little trick of mine is a well-kept secret."

"But people kept getting too close to it," said Jamie. "Art Johnson, and Joseph Woolf, and Cindy Bell, and me. . . "

"Yes," sighed Harry. "Cindy was a pain, although I think I've scared her off. And Pearl kept sniffing around too. She got hold of Vinnie, and was trying to bribe him into talking. . . I had him take the bribe and tell her a pack of lies, so I think that's thrown her off the scent for a while. She's smart, but not as smart as her big brother."

He gave Jamie a fatherly smile. "In fact, the only person smart enough to catch me out, Jamie, is sitting right in front of me."

He fell silent at last, and watched Jamie intently. Jamie tried to rearrange his face into a safe sort of neutral. They sat in silence. The sunlit afternoon felt far away. Somewhere, the very distant traffic rumbled. Somewhere, a busker played a clarinet. They were in a different world.

"Jamie," said Harry. He spoke more softly now. "I know you'll understand. I *had* to do it. For the paper. It was going to go under, kid, TV news was going to ruin us. Six big papers went bust last year. *Six*. Don't you want newspapers to survive?"

"Not like this," said Jamie. "We're meant to tell the truth."

"And I tell the truth, Jamie. Page two onwards is solid honest reporting. That's good enough. That makes it worth it."

"No," said Jamie, "it doesn't." He knew he ought to keep quiet, but he couldn't seem to stop himself. "If you can't run it, give it to Pearl. She would never have done this."

At the mention of his sister's name, Harry Hooper scowled. It was the first face Jamie had ever seen him do that wasn't dignified.

"Do you have any *idea*," he snapped, "any idea at all, how important this paper is? It's just some fairground ride to you." He slammed a fist on the desk. "Get it through your head, kid, that I tell half a million people what to think every morning. I am one of the most powerful people in America. That walking moustache of a chief of police, that idiot of a mayor – do you think they would be anything without me? They do what I say. I *run* this city."

His other fist came crashing down next to his first. Jamie thought he looked a little desperate. "Jamie, I have kept this paper *alive*. If I lose the *Yorker* now, I lose everything. I'd be powerless." His eyes widened. "I could go to jail."

"You deserve to be in jail!" Jamie had lost all self-control now. "Joseph Woolf is in jail, and he didn't do anything. Art Johnson can't get a job. You tried to have me killed! You're the one who thinks it's just a ride, but you're hurting people."

There was a long pause as Harry Hooper surveyed him. The pause was slightly ruined by the busker, who didn't seem to be very good at the clarinet.

"I'm sorry you feel that way, Jamie," said Harry at last. He spoke very, very softly. "I hoped I might be looking at our Young Reporter of the Year. And much more. I see a lot of me in you, kid."

"Are you for real?" exploded Jamie. "Do you think this is a movie? I'm nothing like you. I don't want to be anything like you. You think I'll be quiet if you let me win a stupid *competition*?"

All Harry's softness vanished in an instant. His jaw tightened, and he got up and walked across the office. "Well," he said, "since I can't make you see reason…" He opened the door. "Vinnie. I'm afraid Mr Creeden is being very stubborn."

"Geez. Kids, huh," said Vinnie. And his huge shadow crossed the doorway, followed by the man himself.

"I will leave you two to it," said Harry. He gave Jamie one last wounded look. "Disappointing, Jamie. We could have done great things together. Well. Goodbye.

And thank you once again. You were a very fine paperboy." And with that Harry Hooper left the room, shutting the door behind himself with a genteel click.

Jamie shrank back. The noise of the clarinet seemed to grow in urgency as the busker creaked up another scale outside the window.

A scale?

His mind raced. A busker wouldn't play scales. And, come to think of it, they shouldn't be playing *anything* right outside his window, when he was on the eleventh floor...

He moved fast. By the time Vinnie had crossed the room, Jamie had worked out which window had the ladder, and was on the sill.

The height was dizzying. He crouched on the ledge and stared down. Eve was sitting ten rungs below, one arm looped around the ladder's side, puffing out scales, apparently unconcerned by the height. It was so mad and so typically *Eve* that part of Jamie almost wanted to laugh. But mostly he wanted to not be climbing out of a window eleven floors above street level.

She glanced up. "Come on," she said, giving him an

encouraging bob of the head.

He still hesitated. But then came Vinnie's enormous hands, reaching for his ankles, so he had no choice. He went at full Jamie-Creeden-speed, and began to shimmy down. Below him, Eve stopped playing, and shimmied ahead of him. Vinnie tried to follow, but shimmying was not his forte: in fact, he couldn't get his enormous shoulders through the window. He kept shoving himself stupidly forward, as though that might help.

"You're nearly there! You're doing great!" came Rose's voice. She was at the bottom, holding them in place.

Wrf! agreed Pumpkin, by her feet.

Eve reached the ground, then Jamie. None of them spoke. They collapsed the ladder; the top rungs came cascading over the middle, then the top and middle came cascading over the bottom. Then Eve and Rose picked up either end, and gestured for Jamie to take the middle. Above them, it finally occurred to Vinnie that he might be better off taking the elevator.

"Follow me," said Rose, hoisting her end on to her

shoulder. "Quickly!"

And, staggering under the weight of the ladder, they ran.

MANHATTAN UNIT
ENGINE 10/LADDER 19

2 July 1969

The ladder, of course, belonged to the Midtown Manhattan Firehouse, which housed Engine Company 10 and Ladder Company 19. The firehouse was bright and welcoming, and each of the four new arrivals was thrilled to be there, each for their own reasons.

Rose Johnson was thrilled because she was home. All the firefighters were pleased to see her, and called out as she emerged from between the engines:

"Rose!" "She's back!" "*Now* will you tell us what that ladder was for, little miss?" And they took it in turns to lift her up and swing her in the air. The lifting and swinging got more and more impressive as it went on, and Jamie began to suspect they might be *slightly* showing off.

Eve Hooper-Banks was thrilled because the room was full of interesting engines and exhaust removal systems and pneumatic grabbers and compressed air breathing apparatuses and so on.

Pumpkin was thrilled because he had fallen deeply and irrevocably in love with the Midtown Firehouse dog. It is traditional for New York firehouses to keep a Dalmatian, and this one was particularly beautiful. Unfortunately, she thought that Pumpkin was a cushion, and kept trying to sit on him.

And Jamie Creeden was thrilled because the firehouse didn't involve Harry Hooper, or Vinnie Costa, or being dead. Which was awesome.

The firefighters were the friendliest people he had ever met. They all asked his name and made him welcome, and one came sliding down the pole from the kitchen above with three mugs of cocoa for the children, and a small saucer full of milk for Pumpkin. While Rose explained to them all why she had wanted the ladder, Eve explained to Jamie how Rose had spotted Harry listening in to their phone conversation on the other line, hearing everything that Jamie had found out. When he had then made very flimsy excuses to leave at once, Eve and Rose had slipped out to follow.

"He met Vinnie outside, and Rose recognized him," said Eve. "I figured if Uncle Harry was going to hurt you he'd either have to leave the building, or get you to his office. So Rose suggested we get the ladder, to take a look." She patted her satchel. "And I happened to have my clarinet."

"It was brilliant," Jamie said. "Again. Thank you. And I'm sorry ... about suspecting your mom, and yelling at you, and..."

"Oh, don't be boring." Eve waved her hand. "I'm sorry too, obviously, it all goes without saying. Hurry up and tell me what happened already. We couldn't hear that much outside the window."

So Jamie told her. She listened in silence, as did Rose and a circle of fascinated firefighters.

"It was all lies," Jamie finished. "Everything the *Yorker* stood for…" His voice trailed off, and he realized that his eyes were filling with hot tears as he spoke. He was so *angry*.

"And now," he concluded, "I can't go home … none of us can. And, oh God, my mom will be going back to the apartment tonight. She has no idea about the danger…"

Rose put her arm around him, and from her gangling height, Eve patted him kindly on the head.

"Don't worry, kid," said the captain of the engine company. "We'll call your mom. And we'll find somewhere you can both hide out for a bit."

"That's right," said the captain of the ladder company. "Some place you can lie low for a while, and stay quiet till this all dies down. It'll be all right."

Jamie looked at Eve, who bobbed around in agreement. He looked at Rose, who nodded gravely. He looked at Pumpkin, who was currently trying to climb the firefighters' pole in a bid to reach the Dalmatian's eye level.

"Thank you," he said. "Really. I mean it. But I don't want to be quiet. I don't want this to die down. What about Art?"

"You've tried, Jamie," said Rose, "and I'm really grateful. But it's gotten too dangerous." And all the firefighters murmured sadly in agreement.

"But unless we say something, it will *stay* dangerous," protested Jamie. "We're in danger because we're the only people who know. The only way to change that is to start talking, as loudly as possible and to as many people as possible."

And this was a good point. Slowly, Eve and Rose nodded. The firefighters all nodded. The Dalmatian wagged her tail, accidentally tapping Pumpkin on the head and sending him sliding back down the pole.

"The police, then?" said the captain of the engine company.

The children exchanged glances, thinking of the chief of police. Firstly, he was clearly in Harry's pocket, and secondly, he was mostly made of moustache. "No good," said Jamie. "The chief's afraid of Harry."

"The mayor?" suggested the captain of the ladder company.

"Nope. The mayor was in on the fake shooting. Harry has him just where he wants him."

"Then," said the firefighter next to Jamie, "who *can* we trust?"

And that, of course, was the million-dollar question. Unfortunately, nobody had a million-dollar answer. Gloom hovered over the group, and it threatened to settle. It was impossible to know who was safe.

Then Jamie had an idea. It seemed to him like quite a good idea. And maybe it was a belated wave of vertigo, or maybe it was the sugar in the cocoa, but he suddenly felt giddy with hope. "How about," he said, "we tell half a million people at once?"

"Oh, Jamie, you're in shock," said Rose kindly. "One of the first symptoms of shock," she explained, "is saying things that make absolutely no sense at all."

"Hang on, hear me out," said Jamie. "I can think of a way." He looked around at them all as his idea took shape. He turned to Eve. "Eve, Hal showed us how they make a new metal plate for each page of the paper, every night, and put them in the printing press. The papers come off the press already folded up, and go straight up to the delivery room. If we can replace one of the plates for the *inside* pages, nobody would know, right?"

She nodded thoughtfully. "Sure, that's true…"

"There you go," Jamie said. "We write the story, substitute one of the plates, and tomorrow morning the whole city reads about it in their morning edition of the *Yorker*."

Everybody else was looking at Jamie as though they were still a bit worried about him, but Eve was nodding thoughtfully. "That part's all right. But how do we get past the journalists and Hal?"

If Jamie had learned one thing today, it was that you should always pay attention to the obvious. He looked at the firefighters and the firehouse and the fire engines, and the silent alarm above them all, ready to call them into action. "How about," he said, "we set off the fire alarms?"

And this won the others over at once, and they all said "Ooh" and "Aah" and "Yes!" and "Woof!" and "Wrf". But Eve was still worried.

"That won't give us very long," she pointed out. "Once people see there's no fire, they'll come back in."

"How about we start an actual fire then?" said Jamie. "Just a small one?"

Every firefighter turned to gaze at him in united horror.

"Never mind," he said quickly.

"Why don't we play Harry's own game?" said Rose suddenly. She had been sitting with her knees huddled to her chest, but now she sat up straight. "We can fake it. We don't need a fire. People just need to see smoke."

"No smoke without fire, Rose," said the captain of the engine company, patting her heavily on the shoulder.

"I know. But there's already fire, so there's already smoke. Lots of it. We just need to let some of that smoke out."

Eve and Jamie looked at each other. *The candle.*

There was a lot of appreciative murmuring, as all the firefighters realized what Rose meant. They all began debating how best to go about it. The *Yorker* candle shaft and its design was famous among firefighters, it turned out: partly because it was a wonder of engineering, and partly because it was such a colossally bad idea.

"The smoke goes out of the extractor vent at the top," said Rose. "But if I open one of the emergency vents in the side, it'll leak out. There'll be *loads*. If I open some windows nearby, it'll all start billowing out."

The appreciative murmuring turned more serious, as the firefighters and Rose all debated which vents and hatches she would need to use, and how the smoke would behave, and how to make sure it billowed out of the right places in the right way. Eve listened with interest. Jamie did his best interested face, but it was all quite technical, and he didn't really understand most of it. The more complicated it got, the more his heart sank.

"Rose," he said at last, "are you sure about this? It all sounds a bit . . . difficult."

"Jamie," said Rose. She got off her chair and put her solemn face right up to his, which was a bit alarming. "You know about reporting: I trust you. I know about fire and smoke. You need to trust me. I can do this – for my dad. OK?"

Which was quite moving, except that Pumpkin chose that moment to dive off the ladder he had been climbing, and on to the Dalmatian's head. A lot of confused *woof*ing and *wrf*ing ensued, and in the end they could only be calmed down with a quick dousing from a bucket of water.

When everything had settled again, Eve scooped a bedraggled Pumpkin on to her lap, rubbed him down thoroughly with the edge of her dress and picked up the conversation as though nothing had happened. "If we're going to do this," she said, "we don't have all that much time. We want to get there after most of the plates have been finished, but we don't want to make the paper miss its delivery, or the whole thing will be wasted. So let's say you should come to put the fire out at ten to nine. I'll need seventeen minutes before that to make the plate, I reckon, and we'll need five minutes to get everyone out of the building. So," she concluded, "we need to get ready, really." She stopped towelling down Pumpkin, and inspected him. He now resembled a startled and very soft hedgehog. (It was a good look for him. You could finally see his face. The Dalmatian blinked at him in wonder.)

There was a short silence. The enormity of the task suddenly felt very real. They were walking right back into Harry Hooper's world. Supposing they were caught? Was Vinnie in there still, waiting?

Jamie coughed. "Right," he said. "Let's get ready then."

"Yep," said Rose.

And the firefighters all looked uncertainly at each other; but then the captain of the engine company said, "It's for Art, boys." And nobody could argue with *that*.

"First things first, Jamie," said the captain of the ladder company. "Call your mom at work, and tell her to come here."

Jamie did. He didn't have time to explain everything, and he knew he was scaring her, which felt awful. But he had to warn her.

"Please," he said, "just come here when you finish your shift. Don't go home, whatever you do."

"OK, pet, OK," she said, when Jamie begged her to *swear* it, "I swear, I will. But what's going on? Is everything OK?"

"Not really," said Jamie. He looked around at his friends, and the assembled firefighters, and the joyful dog bundle of Pumpkin and his now-smitten Dalmatian.

"But," he said, "I'm going to make it OK again. By midnight."

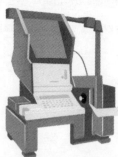

JAMIE CREEDEN REPORTS

2 July 1969

Rose was deep in serious discussion with the firefighters about her plans. Eve was tying thoughtful knots in her hair while she went over and over all the basement's printing machines in her mind, to make sure she knew how they all worked. All Jamie had to do was write the story.

He perched on a chair by himself in the corner of the room, pen and paper in hand, and tried to think anything useful at all.

It is a strange thing, to feel stage fright when nobody

is watching you. But it can happen. If, for example, half a million people are going to read something that you have very little time to write, any or all of the following problems may arise:

1. Every word in the English language will sound stupid in some special way that you have never noticed before.

2. The voice in your head which reads your sentences back to you will start reading them in a stupid voice, so that they all sound rubbish.

3. You will suddenly forget how to spell all words ever.

4. Your hand will stop talking to your brain.

Jamie had all four at once. He had *never* had writer's block. It felt like being deserted by an old friend. So far, he had written:

~~Over the last month~~
~~It was revealed last night~~
~~It is with grave disapointment that this reporter announces~~
~~Kidnap! Arson! Murder!~~
~~Hello, my name is Jamie~~

None of which was much use. And although the fire station was unchangingly bright and calm, Jamie knew that outside, the sun was still drifting west; and at the *Yorker*, the candle was still burning down.

Just then, Eve and Rose appeared on either side of him.

"How's it going?" asked Eve.

"Fine," he said, curving his hand protectively round his notebook. "Just – ah – tweaking it." He looked into their serious faces and sighed miserably. "Actually," he said, "I haven't written anything yet."

"It's going to be all right, Jamie," said Rose. "You're great at this." Only her eyes were visible between her helmet and her enormous fireproof jacket, but they did all the work on behalf of the rest of her face.

"It's like that time we were on the subway tracks, Jamie," said Eve. The knots in her curls bobbed around earnestly. "You can't run. You just have to take it one step at a time."

So Jamie took a deep breath, and tried to forget about all the people who would be reading this and what they would think of it and whether he would be a laughing stock and never allowed to ever print another article ever again and also whether Harry Hooper was going to catch him in the act and call in Vinnie and he and his friends were going to die. And instead, he just wrote the first sentence.

Then he wrote the second.

He started worrying about the fourth then, but he reined himself in, and wrote the third.

Once the ink began curling into place on the page, he was away. He had done this, after all, countless times. It was just another article. What-when-where-who-why-how.

The thing about writing, once it starts going well, is that time suddenly slips along like rapids without you even noticing. And Jamie had a lot to say. This was the story of a lifetime. Once he had put his last triumphant full stop in place, he found it was suddenly time to go. And now it was the others who looked as though their thoughts were racing unhelpfully.

He hugged them both. "We'll be fine," he said. "We'll be *great*. One step at a time."

The three of them spoke very little as they made their way to the *Yorker*. One of the firefighters had already put a ladder up for them in the alley, leading to a window on Ten P.M., which by Eve's calculations was a storage cupboard. The floor *should* be deserted, so that was where Rose would start the smoke. They checked that the alley was empty, then ran down it and clambered up the ladder, and through the window.

They were right: it *was* a storage cupboard. It was mostly full of mops. There was a lot of tripping-over-mops and knocking-over-mops and stepping-in-buckets before they had all found a place to squeeze themselves.

They were a little early. They waited in silence. Jamie counted down the minute on his watch.

"OK," he said. "Time. Good luck, Rose."

Rose nodded in a firm sort of way, but Jamie could see that her hands were shaking. He hoped that it *was* deserted out there; he wished that he was going first, not Rose.

"Hey, you'll be OK," he said, sounding more confident than he felt. "For your dad, remember?"

She nodded, pulled her mask down over her face and

walked out into the corridor.

"Ohmygodohmygodohmygod," said Eve, when the door had shut behind her, "I hope she's OK." She crossed her fingers. "Oh, please don't let her get caught."

"Hey," said Jamie, *"you're* not allowed to be nervous. You're the girl who sets fire to herself and walks on subway tracks and plays clarinets on ladders." Jamie thought that if *Eve* panicked now, he might lose it entirely.

"Oh sure," said Eve. "But it's different watching someone else do something dangerous, you know?"

And Jamie did know. Sending tiny Rose Johnson off into the bowels of the *Yorker* alone felt like pushing a baby bird out of the nest in the vague hope it knew how to fly.

An awful minute of silence passed. Jamie realized he was hugging the mop.

Then the alarm wailed. Jamie was sure that he could smell smoke.

"Oh, well done, Rose, well done," whispered Eve. And the two of them began the three-minute countdown they had agreed on, to give everyone time to leave the building. It turned out that Jamie said "Telephone" in between seconds and Eve said "Elephant", but they said them at the same speed, so it was fine. From below they heard the crowd of press workers tramping up from the basement, muttering and murmuring; then the crowd thinned; then there was quiet.

"Ready?" said Jamie, when the three minutes was up.

"Ready," said Eve.

They stepped out into the deserted hallway. They could feel at once the massive emptiness of the building around them. Twenty-four floors stood in silence. Without all the people and the noise, the glowing brass and gold of the *Yorker* felt like some great temple, to an especially grand sort of god.

So far, so good. Now it was over to Jamie and Eve to make the switch in time for the delivery. "Twenty-seven minutes," said Jamie; and Eve nodded.

They spiralled downwards, past the abandoned reception, on into the basement.

The room stood in disarray. By the linotype machines, lines of finished lead type lay on the tables in their trays. Stacks of paper proofs lay discarded. At the machines themselves, still-pungent coffee cups and ashtrays bore witness to the workers who had sat at them only moments before.

Eve found an empty composing tray, then stood by to help work the tricksy linotype machine. Jamie sat on its stool, and got out his rough copy.

He hit the first key. There was an almighty tap and rattle and clunk, as the linotype moved the letter into place. He clattered out his whole first line. Somehow, he didn't quite believe that the bizarre contraption would work. But then the machine spat a bar of lead out, and those were his words, right there, clear as day.

After that, he typed like a maniac.

Every time he finished a line of type, the machine spat it out, and Eve took it to the composing tray and slotted it in place. Jamie was soon lost in the cacophony of the machine, and the slippery time-rapids that happen when writing is going well. Everything else was forgotten. It was exhilarating.

It was only when he had hit the last full stop, and one last slug of lead had rattled from the machine to be put in place, that he came back to earth. He checked his watch: they were on track.

While Eve took the lead to make a metal plate, he ran to the printing press, to find the plate they were going to replace. They had agreed that page five would be a good one. Safely inside the paper, but near enough to the front that people would still be sure to read it.

Each compartment of the printer took an enormous heave to open, and there were lines and lines of rollers in its guts, all full of metal plates. They had timed it perfectly: every plate was in there, ready to go. They were numbered with black ink, and it didn't take long to find number five.

Then there was nothing to do but wait, and try not to touch anything. These were not Jamie's strong suits, and he had never felt so very full of fidget as he did now. He checked his watch roughly every three seconds, and chewed his bottom lip furiously, and danced a very tiny jig of impatience. Every half-heard sound made him jump.

Outside, sirens wailed; and a minute later, Rose came tapping down to the basement. She held out her hand for a high five, but it was still a very shaky hand, so the high five wobbled a bit.

"Good job, Rose," said Jamie. "All OK up there? Firefighters are in?"

"Yup," she said. And she smiled a wobbly smile. "They're having a great time, running around yelling like it's the end times, and spraying each other with the hoses. Eve not done yet?"

Jamie shook his head, and checked his watch yet again. Where *was* she?

But at last Eve returned with a curved metal plate, the number five marked on it in black ink.

"Well done, good, brilliant, great," said Jamie. "Yes, cool, OK."

Eve ignored this, which was sensible. "Where do you want it?"

So Jamie took out the original – "Sorry, Ted," he whispered, as he removed his piece on the Unacceptable Situation with the Trash Collection – and Eve put Jamie's article in. She closed the machine again and patted its side. "OK," she said. "We're done."

The three of them did one last sweep of the room. Eve took all the slugs back out of the composing tray and stuffed them in her pocket. Jamie put Ted's plate in a big kit bag they had brought from the fire station, and slung it over his shoulder. They all looked carefully, but they couldn't see any other signs of their presence.

They went to the lobby, and eventually managed to flag down the captain of the ladder company, once he had finished entirely covering the captain of the engine company in foam. "All done?" he said, and they nodded. "OK," he yelled to the others, "party's over! Tyrone, Pedro, shut the vents – everybody out!"

Eve and Jamie were given firefighter's jackets and helmets to put on, just like Rose's. Jamie pulled his low over his telltale red hair, making sure it was all firmly tucked away. Then the three children left one at a time, helmets slung low over their faces. They each left with one of the firefighters, so that they could blend in. And if they were a *bit* smaller than average, the crowds milling around outside were too hypnotized by all the smoke and pandemonium to notice.

They slunk quickly into the belly of a waiting engine, where the firefighters joined them, one by one.

Then the engines thrummed, the sirens blared, and they pulled away from it all. Away from the *Yorker*;

away from the crowds of pressmen, gawping and gossiping; and away from Harry Hooper, who watched the smoke with great unruffled dignity, head on one side. Considering.

SAFETY

2 July 1969

When they were back at the fire station, the three children tumbled out of the engine into an exhausted hug, and all spoke at once. "Do you think it worked?" "Do you?" "Did you make the plate?" "Do you think they'll notice?" "Did he see us?" "Are you OK?" "Are *you*?"

The trouble with this particular conversation was that everybody was asking questions, and nobody was answering them. So the questions just piled up, and the three soot-covered friends stayed tangled up together repeating their questions at each other, and confusion reigned.

And then a question came from outside the hug.

"Jamie, pet? Are you all right? What's going on?"

Jamie disentangled himself, and with a sob, he threw his arms around the small, tired, red-headed woman who now stood among the engines in the bright safety of the firehouse. And she hugged him very tightly back.

His mom was here. Safe. Vinnie couldn't touch her. And he could *finally* tell her everything.

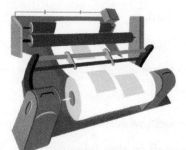

THE *YORKER* GOES TO PRINT

2 July 1969– 9.30 p.m. precisely

Things were back to normal inside the *Yorker*, except that they were all working a bit quicker than usual. In the print room, Hal was rushing through his usual inspection of all the plates, at 9.29.

At plate five, he paused. He frowned. He rubbed his belly uncertainly.

"Quickly, man, quickly!" called Harry. "Is there a problem?"

Hal hesitated. Then he put back plate number five, with a heavy clunk.

"No, boss," he said. And he started up the press.

It came to life with a great rumble, at 9.30 on the dot. It shuddered. It roared. The room shook. And as the conveyer belt whirred to life, and papers sailed upwards, the staff in the delivery room above began instantly to sort them into boxes. Fire or no fire, half a million papers had to be sent out into the world by midnight, to meet the trains and vans that waited for them, to be taken to hundreds of stores, to be picked up by children on bicycles, to reach the stoops and mailboxes of eager readers by 7.30 without fail.

Harry clapped Hal on the back. "Punctual," he said. "Punctual! That's what I like to see."

"Yes, boss," said Hal. And although his hand shook very slightly, he was smiling. "Punctual," he agreed, "and accurate."

IN CASE YOU
WERE WONDERING

2 July 1969

Vinnie had been spending most of this time lurking in Jamie's apartment. He and the cockroach made friends, which was nice for the cockroach, who had been missing Cindy's heel for many cockroach years. Otherwise, it was an uneventful wait. At around three a.m. Vinnie Costa gave up, hurtled his car home through the deserted streets and went to bed. There was, he told himself, no rush.

After all, what harm could the boy do in one night?

ALWAYS PUNCTUAL

3 July 1969

They all slept on the bunks in the firehouse that night. This was difficult, because at intervals the alarm would wail and the firefighters would pile into their engines and drive off, sirens blaring. But Jamie was very, very tired, which helped.

He woke a little earlier than usual. The night shift firefighters were on their way out, and the morning shift were arriving and grumbling their way towards coffee. Jamie checked his watch.

Then he sprang up, left the others a note, left the firehouse behind and went pedalling back over Brooklyn Bridge, over the silvered waters of the East River, back to Bay Ridge and Lou Moon's convenience store. He had papers to deliver. And he wouldn't miss this route for the world.

The bell played a small symphony of exuberance as he slammed open the door. Lou's moustache fluttered in the breeze. He looked up with eyes full of soulful sorrow, and opened his mouth to complain, but Jamie said such an enthusiastic "Good morning!" that he shut it again.

Jamie ripped the front four pages of the *Yorker* open. And there it was:

THIS PAPER IS LYING TO YOU

By Jamie Creeden

The Yorker's own Harry Hooper has been faking sensashunal events across New York for the last year in order to sell more papers, it emerged last night. The stories have all been printed under the name Bud Finkleby, but were penned by Mr Harry Hooper himself.

Irena Dragunova does not exist and was never at the Angel Theatre. The Arsonist is never really there among his flames: they are electrical fires which have been planted several hours earlier, and the voice is a recording. No one tried to shoot the mayor: Harry Hooper fired his own gun into the wall. These stories were all invented by Harry Hooper, desperate to keep his sales up with ever more sensashunal stories.

This reporter has been thretened for his knowledge of this secret. If any harm comes to Jamie Creeden, Rose Johnson, Eve Hooper-Banks or their loved ones, you will all know who did it.

Police should closely examin all stories in the Yorker that finish after nine thirty at night. As the makers of the Printomatic 440 can confirm, the press has a maximum speed of two hundred thousand papers an hour. And as the delivery drivers can confirm, the five hundred thousand nightly copies of the Morning Yorker have never been late for collection at midnight. I call on readers to do the math. This means that all these stories had to go to print before they had happened. How is this possible? Because Harry Hooper already knew that they would go ahead!

We need an investigation now! The chief of police is in Hooper's pocket and cannot be trusted with the job. The mayor lied about getting shot. We must all ask questions in their place, since they have failed us!

We do not know who we can trust, and so we trust in the people of the United States of America. We call on you to speek for us. We know you believe that papers should tell the truth. You have been lied to. Demand a full investigation immediately! Thank you. And good luck.

It was all there, and out in the world. They had done it.

"Thanks, Lou!" said Jamie. "Bye!" He loaded up his satchel and whirled back out again.

Lou watched him, puzzled. Then he shrugged, and sighed, and concluded: "Strange kid."

But Jamie was not around to hear this assessment of himself. He was already riding through the gathering dawn, down the straight wide streets, tearing round their sharp corners, delivering the *Morning Yorker* to the tower blocks and town houses of Brooklyn, New York City.

And when he had finished, he pulled page five out from a spare copy of the paper. He wrote a quick note with his name and address and telephone number, and put it all in an envelope. Then he went to the post office, and submitted his entry for the Young Reporter of the Year 1969.

PAGE FIVE IS A HIT!

3 July 1969

Once word got around about page five, the *Yorker* flew off the shelves. Every copy had been sold by ten a.m., and after that people had to borrow one or steal one or read one over the shoulders of strangers on the subway. Everyone was agog to read the story by the young reporter who was taking on Harry Hooper himself.

At first the chief of police hid behind his moustache; and the mayor issued a statement saying that he had no comment, and had no intention of having a comment, and everyone should stop calling and leave him alone.

But by the end of the day the outrage had grown too big to ignore, and the president himself was demanding an investigation.

After that, everything began to unravel.

Grandfather Hooper sacked Harry Hooper and handed the management of the *Yorker* over to Pearl, who immediately began a thorough investigation into the newspaper, and put every waking hour into making sure it was now run properly.

This had the wonderful, unexpected side effect that she no longer had any time to deal with Eve.

"We've never gotten along so well," Eve told the others, dazed. "She didn't even notice that I hadn't brushed my hair." It took three days for the evidence to mount against the mayor, but in the end he confessed, and Joseph Woolf was released with a presidential apology. Jamie joined the crowds of reporters waiting to meet him, because he was writing up the story for the *Bay Ridge Bugle*. It felt good to be working for his own paper again; he had big plans for the first issue of the fall term. He had to jostle for his space, and everyone else was a lot taller and shinier than him, which made it tricky.

But when Woolf appeared, he ignored the crowd, and went straight to shake Jamie's hand. He bared his teeth in a jack-o'-lantern grin. "Tell the other little billy goats that Joseph says hello," he said. "My luck changed when you walked in. And tell them that I won. One-hundred-and-thirty-six-thousand-three-hundred-and-twenty-nine heads to one-hundred-and-thirty-six-thousand-three-hundred-and-twenty-eight tails."

So Jamie did tell them, that very afternoon, as they lay in Central Park. They had been walking Pumpkin and the Dalmatian, whose name was apparently Cynthia. Now they were lying on their backs under an oak tree, while the dogs tried to make friends with a frankly uninterested squirrel.

Art had been given his job back at the firehouse, but Rose seemed subdued. She hadn't been herself since the night in the *Yorker*, but when the others asked what was on her mind, she would only ever tell them about some neighbour who was sick or some friend who was unhappy. As they lay there that afternoon, she finally said what she was really worrying about; but she said it so quietly that Jamie thought he might have just heard an overexuberant ant.

Eve helpfully said, "What?", so Rose repeated herself, more loudly:

"I don't think I want to be a firefighter."

"Well, that's OK," said Jamie. "You're allowed to change your mind."

"I know," said Rose, blinking up at the clouds that were shape-shifting above. "It's just, I always believed I'd be brave. And as soon as the heat and smoke started coming out, I was really scared. I knew I was safe, but I was scared anyway." She sighed. "I'm not brave at all."

Jamie remembered how her hand had trembled as they high-fived. He rolled over on to his front, propped up on his elbows so that he could look at her properly. "You *were* brave!" he said. "You were scared, but you did the job anyway. That's brave."

"But," she said, big eyes glistening, "I never want to do anything like it ever again, ever."

"I always thought it was weird that you wanted to

be a firefighter," Eve chipped in.

"Um," said Jamie, "Eve—"

"Because," Eve ploughed on, "you're so obviously a different sort of brave. You let yourself care about other people all the time, even when it hurts. Most people can't do that. You're brave like nurses and carers and that man who runs the soup kitchen on Third Avenue."

Rose still sniffed uncertainly. But her eyes widened a bit, as if they were thinking a new thought for the first time. Above her, the clouds gently shifted and rearranged themselves.

"What about you, Jamie?" said Eve. "Do you still want to be a reporter, after everything that happened?"

Jamie had been thinking about this. A lot of the time, the past week had been terrifying, or lonely, or both. And the world of news reporting was a lot more complicated than he had expected. He was still shaken by Harry Hooper – and the mayor, and the chief of police – and there would always be more power-hungry people like them, willing to lie and cheat. Trying to report the truth would be a lot more exhausting than he'd bargained for.

But. He had met new people and seen new places and felt new feelings and never once sat still, and he wanted to live a life that was as frantically *alive* as that, always.

"Yeah," he said. "Yeah, I really do."

"Good," said Eve. "Because if you don't win Young Reporter, I will eat my hat." She thought about this, then added, "Actually, I don't have a hat. I will eat some of Mother's hats, she has loads."

And although it isn't very modest to be sure you are the best young reporter in all of the United States of America, it was difficult for Jamie to disagree. *Everyone* expected him to win.

Which is why it was quite a surprise when, the next morning, Sidney Blake's article interviewing the head of the FBI appeared on the front page of the *Yorker*, with a rosette printed over it saying WINNER.

He was the first child ever to win the competition two years in a row. There was a note printed alongside the article, explaining that he deserved this honour for his prestigious interviews, his polite interview questions and his immaculate spelling.

That morning Jamie and Rose had been due to meet Eve at the *Yorker*, where she had spent the morning with Pearl. As they *fwmph*ed through the door, mother and daughter were coming downstairs.

"It wasn't even good journalism!" Eve was shouting. "Did you read it? They spent half the interview talking about his favourite ice cream flavour. Which is strawberry, in case anyone cared, which literally no one does."

"Don't *shout*, Eve," Pearl said. "Really! I know you're upset that I didn't give your friend a prize. But this is *embarrassing*."

At this point, Rose stepped in and put a hand on Eve's arm. "Please, Ms Hooper-Banks," Rose said gently. "We're all a bit upset. We just don't understand. Jamie's article was revolutionary."

"Jamie's article," began Pearl – and then she saw Jamie, and turned to him. "*Your* article, dear, might have been sensational. But it was also a poorly spelled, impertinent lot of . . . of *noise*." She straightened her blouse. "And frankly, I don't want that story to garner any more publicity. The sooner New York forgets the disgrace to our family, the better."

"Mother, Uncle Harry disgraced us, not Jamie," said Eve, and "Oh, I hadn't thought of it like that, this must be really hard for you," said Rose.

"Rose, dear," said Pearl, "I don't need your sympathy. Please stop trying to be nice to me. And you would all do well to stop trying to be so smart, and remember that you are just small children, who are making far too much noise." Everyone in the foyer was watching them. Even the receptionist wasn't entirely bored by the situation.

Pearl took a deep breath. Then she said, "Jamie. Rose. Please leave the premises. Now."

"Fine," said Jamie.

"Fine," said Rose.

"I'm going too," said Eve.

And they left the *Morning Yorker* behind them: *Fwmph. Fwmph. Fwmph.*

Outside, they blinked stupidly in the sunlight.

It was Rose who spoke first. "Why," she asked, baffled, "would you *not* want people to try and be smart and nice?"

"It gets in the way," said Eve bitterly. "People like Mother and Uncle Harry want everyone to be stupid and selfish and quiet, so we don't notice when things aren't fair, and if we do notice we don't care, and if we do notice and we do care then we don't say anything."

There was a silence at that. Or rather, because there is never a silence in New York, there was a moment when all they heard was the ever-present busy hum of the city, as eight million people went from here to there and from there to here, built things up and tore them down again, learned things and forgot them and rediscovered them, fought battles and won them and lost them and tried again. In the bright sunlight, everybody who bustled past looked very beautiful – even the stupid and selfish and quiet ones.

"Well," said Jamie. He bent down to unlock his bike. "That's tough. Because *I* reckon we're going to keep making noise."

He considered this, straightened up and added: "A lot of really, really, really *loud* noise."

And the three children got on their bicycles and cycled away up Fifth Avenue, and the lights were green and green and green and green, all the way down.

EXTRA! EXTRA!

We could perhaps leave them there, speeding along that avenue. But there is one more thing that I think you should know about, because it is quite extraordinary.

That evening, the children all went to Pepe's to watch Cindy Bell. She was running a full special on the events since Jamie's report, including an interview with Jamie that he had recorded with her the day before. In the week of the *Yorker*'s disgrace, her ratings had shot up again, and she had been given her full hour back.

Pepe gave everyone free chocolate milkshakes

to celebrate Jamie's first TV appearance. When he appeared on the screen, they all whooped and cheered.

The whole show was brilliant – Cindy was back to her old self. But the best bit came just before the weather, when she turned to the camera, looking like a *particularly* serious Mr Whippy ice cream.

"And before we take a look at the forecast, we've just got time to congratulate Sidney Blake, who today won the *Yorker*'s prestigious Young Reporter of the Year competition for the second year in a row. Sidney's piece, an interview with director of the FBI Mark McMackerel, was praised for being 'polite' and having 'immaculate spelling.' Congratulations, Sidney – I'm sure I speak for all of my viewers tonight when I wish you well."

Eve and Rose made sympathetic noises, and Pepe topped up Jamie's milkshake. He took a big swallow and tried not to mind.

"However."

Everyone looked back at the screen.

"There has been some discussion in the *Goodnight, New York* studio about the prize," Cindy went on. "In our opinion it is a scandal that the prize did not go to Jamie

Creeden, who submitted his brave and groundbreaking report on the activities of former *Morning Yorker* editor Harry Hooper. His commitment to the truth is an example to all of us in the press. We are here to tell the truth, even about powerful people – *especially* about powerful people. I know that I for one was looking forward to reading his articles over the next year, and I am sure that others share my disappointment."

On the TV screen, Cindy Bell frowned out at them all. Across New York, people nodded in agreement. In Pepe's diner, four watchers sat forward on the edges of their seats, mouths open.

"But I have good news," Cindy went on. "If anybody would like to hear more from this intrepid young reporter, they can subscribe to his own paper. The *Bay Ridge Bugle* is available weekly for twenty cents a copy. Viewers wishing to subscribe should call the number now showing at the bottom of their screens." And a number flashed up in red on the TV, with the words CALL NOW!

"And now," said Cindy calmly, "for the weather."

And while she explained that it was probably going

to be sunny, being summer and all, Eve and Rose and Jamie all exploded with chatter and amazement and some slightly uncontrolled splutters of chocolate milkshake. Pepe made another round of milkshakes, because he couldn't think of any other way to express his delight.

After the weather, Cindy concluded, "So, all in all, it's July. And meanwhile, I'm told that subscriptions to the *Bay Ridge Bugle* have been pouring in. Jamie, sweetie, if you're watching, and I bet you are: we might need to find you a proper printing press."

And this made everyone in the diner go entirely nuts, for ages and ages and ages.

And *that* is how Jamie Creeden, who had always known he was going to write the news, turned out – quite unexpectedly – to be right.

ACKNOWLEDGEMENTS

Many people helped to make this book punctual and accurate and other good things, so I have some very important *thank yous* to say.

For the beautiful object you now hold, I am indebted to Marco Guadalupi for the illustrations, and to Andrew Biscomb and Bleddyn Sion for the design.

For the story inside it, my thanks to a trio of editors – Sophie Cashell and Lauren Fortune for helping it on its way, and Genevieve Herr for steering it so ably home. Thanks also to Jessica White and Pete Matthews for the heroic copy-editing. And thanks, as always, to Sam Plumb and Dylan Townley for their insightful comments, from Central Park chats to London read-throughs.

Endless gratitude to my agent, Bryony Woods, who is tireless and astonishing.

And finally, a great transatlantic thank you to Erin Simmons and Tanner Efinger, for making me so welcome in New York. I miss you!

Sylvia Bishop lives in London with a motley crew of friends and lamps. She is the author of *Erica's Elephant*, *The Bookshop Girl* and *The Secret of the Night Train*, and her books have been translated into thirteen languages.

Follow Sylvia on Twitter @SylviaBishop

Marco Guadalupi is a digital artist from Brindisi,
a little sea town in Southern Italy. Before becoming
an illustrator he was a writer, and has always
enjoyed telling stories.

Follow Marco on Twitter @marcoguadalupi

Also available:

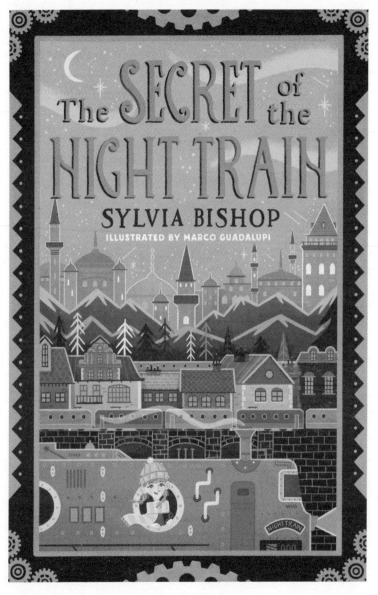